Ten Mir

Cover image "Cam" is a derivative of "attack-blackmailing-crime-criminal-1840256/" by Pexels. "Cam" is licensed under the Creative Commons Attribution-NonCommercial-NoDerivatives 4.0 International (CC BY-NC-ND 4.0) by Joe Mansour

This work is licensed under the Creative Commons Attribution-NonCommercial-NoDerivatives 4.0 International (CC BY-NC-ND 4.0) by Joe Mansour

This is a work of fiction. Names, characters, businesses, places, events and incidents are either the products of the author's imagination or used in a fictitious manner. Any resemblance to actual persons, living or dead, or actual events is purely coincidental.

Visit jemansour.com for more information.

Also by Joe Mansour.

Calhoun:Sacrifice

Calhoun: Retribution

For Shelley, my heart and everything attached.

Contents

One..7
Minus Ten...15
Two..25
Minus Nine..38
Three..42
Minus Eight..52
Four..73
Minus Seven..85
Five...111
Minus Six..124
Six...140
Minus Five..152
Seven..169
Minus Four...177
Eight...182
Minus Three...193
Nine..201
Minus Two..212
Ten..222
Minus One..229
 Acknowledgements.....................................235

One

The door of Sharpe's Gun Emporium swung open, setting the bell to jangling. Trevor Sharpe, glanced up from the piece he was reassembling, his face a mask of benign greeting hiding the annoyance that commerce had intruded on his pleasure. He laid a cloth over the wonderful machine that he had been stripping down to degrease and then re-oil. Or weapon of death, as Mrs Sharpe called them, evil things that she wouldn't allow in the house, even though they paid for her idle life, enabled her to waste it at coffee mornings and beauty parlours. No wonder he always worked late, there was nothing at home for him except sarcastic comments and bitter whining about how other husbands provided more for their wives. Well, where was his incentive? She sat on her arse all day, except when a Swedish hunk was rubbing some of the fat from it. Probably fucking her as well, they were all fucking her except him, God knows he wasn't getting any, that frigid cow was always tired when he got in, though from what he couldn't work out, it wasn't as if they had children, that sterile bitch hadn't given him any, no one to pass the business on to when he died. She would sell up and go off cruising round the world fucking cabin boys and anyone else who would have her.

But here was a customer, a decent enough looking young man, black hair brushed back in a sensible cut, brown boots and blue jeans, wearing a large coat despite it being a warm day, but maybe that's what the fashion was now? A rucksack strap over his right shoulder, the bag squashed up, empty. Unlikely that he could afford a gun, but you never know, he might at least buy a knife.

"Can I help you?" Sharpe asked, rising from his seat, forcing a smile on to his dour face, arms spread out indicating his wares.

"I'll help myself." The man answered pulling out a pistol from under his parka.

The first two shots hit Sharpe in the chest, pushing him backwards, arms flailing out, toppling the chair as he lurched back. The third to the head, spraying blood, brains and bone onto the glass fronted cabinets behind him. Legs giving way, he collapsed slumping to the ground, his expression slack around the hole in his face.

His murderer turned to lock the door, with a quick glance outside he flipped the 'Welcome' sign over to 'Closed'. He pulled the suppressor free letting it drop to the floor, returned the automatic to its holster under his left armpit, and walked round the counter to the corpse. Bending to frisk the twitching body he found a set of keys in a trouser pocket. Using one to unlock the main display he took from it two machine pistols and placed them on the counter. The cabinet behind held empty magazines and cartons of armour piercing rounds. He primed the auto loader, feeding in the clips and pouring the cartridges into the hopper. It whirred into life, loading the magazines, full ones dropping onto the tray below it. He loaded the guns with the first two, chambering a round in each, and dropped them into his coat's large poacher pockets, filled the hand warmer pockets with the rest. Satisfied he switched the machine off and stepped back over the corpse, crushing the suppressor under a foot on his route to the door.

Outside the street was deserted, the restricted shops were located in the seedier part of town, the passing traffic, few and far between at 10 in the morning, limited to that heading to or from the super casino, or visiting the brothels and drug dens that accreted to it.

He climbed on to the motorbike he had parked outside and pulled out, cutting down side alleys and across roads heading for the high-street. Here the traffic was busier and he weaved amongst the cars until he was able to pull up in a loading bay outside the First Municipal bank.

He kicked down the stand and swung off, pushed his left hand in to a pocket and entered the building.

Inside, he waited for the automatic doors to slide shut and flicked the switch to lock them in place. The interior was laid out to give the impression of casual informality, pot plants and padded chairs, belied by the tellers at one end behind bulletproof glass conducting business via speaker grille. He looked round the room counting the guards. Two, a man near the counter, in his sixties, his uniform pressed, sharp creases in the trousers, a friendly smile on his face, making small talk with the customers. The other, a woman, late twenties, hair tied back under an ill fitting hat. Watching the entrance she had noticed his actions and was coming over to admonish him. The bleak monotony of her day broken, she rested her hands on her hips over truncheon and revolver, a provocative warning for him not to try anything, not to give her any lip and she might go easy on him. Be something to tell Mike tonight as they ate tea. How she'd caught some lad messing around with the doors and told him off. How he'd looked at her respectfully and apologised, no ma'am he wouldn't do it again. How when they had kids they would bring them up right. She would watch his face when she said that, see his reaction, they'd only been together three months but she felt this was the one. The bank wouldn't keep her on when she was pregnant, not as a guard anyway. She could get a job at the casino watching the monitors, they let you sit down for that. She would be near Mike then, she could watch him working the roulette table taking the dole from the desperate. Yes, she'd mention kids, see if he panicked. She'd cook him something nice, perhaps best not to mention this lad, she didn't want him to think they could be a handful. She opened her mouth to speak, face set in a firm expression, faltering at the sight of the machine pistol he pulled from a pocket, racked back the slide and shot her in the chest.

He fired at the other guard, a diagonal spray from hip to throat reducing the old man to a juddering meat puppet twitching on the floor.

The customers stood in mute shock, open mouthed, unable to process what had just happened, he shouted into the silence.

"Get on the fucking floor! Get on it now!"

Punched the nearest person to him in the stomach, kicked their legs out dropping them. 'Control the situation' Cam said, 'don't give them chance to panic, if you do then you've lost it'.

"On the floor!"

He raised the gun, another burst straight up stitching a line across the ceiling, showering plaster, focusing their minds, the ensuing quiet punctuated by a clatter of shells on the tiles. Terrified they dropped to the ground, faces pressed against the cold marble floor. He scanned them looking for heroes. Satisfied he lowered his arm letting the machine pistol hang at his side, and strode over to the tills where one cashier was still visible sitting behind the bulletproof glass.

"The money." He said, swinging his rucksack off his shoulder and onto the counter.

"OK, Sir, if you will just be patient." The teller said, his face grey, feeling sick, this wasn't like the training video they'd been shown, that hadn't prepared him for this. 'Stay behind the glass' it had said 'You're safe behind the glass, press the alarm and wait for the police. Stay calm, the police will be there soon, play for time if you can but don't put people at risk.'

"I'm not a patient man." The bank robber said, raised the

pistol and shot the first guard in the head.

"Next it's a customer."

Screams that turned to muffled whimpers when he added. "Quiet or I'll pick you."

The cashier froze, unsure what to do. Poor Amy, there was no need for that, no need for such violence, he wasn't going to get away with it, the police would be here soon, he pressed his knee against the alarm again. But what happens then? He'd take hostages, he'd kill more, there was no doubt about that, this man was ruthless, what would make someone act like that? And so young, he didn't even look out of his teens. There was no respect in the world any more, that's what Ted always said. Poor Ted, lying there gasping, hands on his stomach trying to keep his guts in. His pension not enough to make ends meet he'd taken the security job at the bank, hard on a man of his age standing all day, but you never heard him complain, always a smile for the clients. Maybe he'd get some compensation for this, be able to buy that static caravan out by Angus the Expectant, the park with the regular hopper to the casino, free coffee and toasties as long as you kept pumping the slots. What should he do? 'You're safe behind the glass' he didn't feel safe, he glanced to his left where Geoff was cowering on the floor. He should have dropped as well but he was a senior teller and the video had been emphatic on that, 'Stay in view, you must control the situation, try to reason with the assailant, do not tell them that all is hopeless - you don't want to panic them.' Panic them! This man didn't look the type to panic, he looked like he was just out to do some shopping, his face was expressionless, dead, cold blue eyes staring at him. He didn't think he could cope, he should have got down on the floor, let Jessica handle it, she was more senior, where was Jessica? He looked around trying to spot her, all the other seats were vacant.

"The money." The robber said, tapping on the glass with his

gun.

"Of course." The teller opened the till and began taking notes out, pushed the money through the gap under the window to the thief.

'Fracture their world and then give them order' Cam had demonstrated that many times, hammered the lesson home, done it to him, moulded him in to this, a cold blooded killer. He filled the rucksack, buckling it shut, threaded his arms through the straps and hoisted it on to his back. Ignoring the rest of the cash spilling over the counter he walked towards the doors.

"Stay down!" He shouted.

He flicked the switch letting them open again, left without looking back.

Outside a siren wail grew louder, building as a police car came tearing towards the bank. He emptied a pistol into it, the magazine dropping free, the vehicle careened off the road and smashed into a shop front window. Satisfied, he reloaded and returned the gun to his pocket, climbed on to the bike, thumbed the ignition, roaring off up the street.

At the intersection he cut left, followed by a left down the alley that ran behind the bank, keeping his speed down, emerging at the end of the block, pulling out on to the street, in between three fucking police cars! He gunned the bike and weaved amongst them, pulled across the oncoming traffic and down the alley opposite. Came out at the end and turned left again then through two crossroads and another left. Up the street heading out of town, a police car coming the opposite way, lights strobing, siren dopplering. It slowed, turning to cut off his escape. He accelerated and swerved around it, sticking two fingers up at the cops inside. Opened the throttle and sped away, weaving through the traffic kicking at the side of cars to warn them he was there, pushing the bike to its limit.

Two more police cars burst out of the next junction coming up close, a helicopter wouldn't be far behind. This part of the plan wasn't going as well as he'd hoped.

He pulled out a pistol and sprayed the road behind him without looking back. Tyres squealed, sounded like he had hit something, he glanced over his shoulder to check, wobbled, almost dropped the gun.

A lorry at the crossroads ahead was turning right, long and slow. He slammed on his brakes, no time to stop or even turn, the back wheel sliding out. He hooked his left leg over and hunkered down, riding the bike as it slid under the flat-bed grinding to a stop on the other side. He pulled it back upright and revved it. His foot unable to find the gear shift he glanced down at it, useless, twisted out of shape, stuck in third. He dumped the bike, looking around, the haulier climbing down from the cab, sound of sirens building, people stopping to stare, the truck driver swearing at him, he didn't need this.

"Shut your fucking mouths!"

Raised the pistol, swinging it back and forth causing panic, people screaming, some frozen, others running away.

He ran down the nearest side street, cut across another and then down an alley strewn with tramps and rubbish, scrambled over the fence at the end and turned right. Trying to think of a way out of this. Steal a car? Hide out? Shit shit SHIT SHIT SHIT!

He bent over, trying to get his breath back, slow his breathing, override the panic he was feeling.

He straightened, returned the pistol to his pocket, fished a cigarette out and lit it. Looked around weighing up his options.

A C.F. cab was idling at the curb, chrome and metallic purple, armoured tires and bulletproof glass. He pressed a wad of notes against the passenger window and heard the rear door unlock, wrenched it open and climbed in.

"1823 Mary the Hopeful." He said through the grille that separated him from the driver.

"Council kid eh?" The cabbie said. "Hop in, lot of cops

around, we'll take the scenic route."

Minus Ten

The first time John saw Cam was on his way home from school. After an elaborate handshake, he left his mates Tel and Chancy to cut down the back way that would bring him out on the road leading up to his house on the Jeremiah estate. Scrolling through FJOD on his Perse looking for jokes to repost on his Chekme page he rounded the corner where the road bordered a stretch of waste land, a disused warehouse falling in to disrepair, the chain link fence surrounding it having more holes than a colander, made by opportunistic scrappers and the more adventurous youth. The route so familiar he could walk it blindfolded, or at least paying it minimal attention, he kept his eyes on the screen, captivated by the virtual world until a shout made him re-engage with the real. A grunt, the thwack of a blow, a fight taking place. Common sense urged him to move on, curiosity kept him rooted to the spot watching the scene taking place on the wasteground before him.

A woman in her late thirties, dressed in jeans and a T-shirt, long black hair tied back from her face. A man lay unconscious on the ground, two others circled, waiting for an opportunity to strike. One of the men leapt at her, his arms swinging wildly, she stepped to the side and kicked hard at his knee, he crumpled and she smashed her elbow into his face. The other took his chance, John shouted out a warning too late to prevent the fist slamming in to her mouth. Cam reeled back from the punch, struck out with her heel, a blow to the nuts that doubled the man over, then stepped in to grab his head and pulled it down onto her knee. Her attacker collapsing, she spun back springing on the balls of her feet looking round for threats. She lowered her hands, and focused on John.

"Thanks for the warning kid." Her voice husky, accent giving the words a strange inflection, she spat blood onto the concrete, wiped her mouth with the back of her hand.

"Are, are you OK?" He said.

"Fine, just a minor disagreement, he got in a good hit this one."

She looked down at the unconscious man then kicked him hard in the face.

"Not good enough though."

'God, she's beautiful' he thought, watching her breasts heave from the exertion. The way she moved had been poetry, graceful, sleek, vicious and now she stood in front of him in tight jeans that made him desperate to see her arse.

"I live just over there."

He pointed in the general direction of his house. She frowned, a puzzled expression on her face.

"If you want to get cleaned up?" He said.

She stared at him, he seemed harmless, he was sixteen maybe seventeen, average looking, a strong face rather than handsome, brown hair in school regulation cut, wondered what his angle was, whether a kid that young even had an angle. She needed a breather, some time to be able to stop and plan rather than just react, might be an idea to get off the street, go to this boy's house, take it from there.

"Where?"

She walked towards him, slow, lithe, fluid, he could feel his cock hardening, his face flushing from the realisation that she might be able to see it pressing against his trousers.

"Uh, uh, this way."

Turning was awkward, he felt the heat increase in his cheeks, gave an embarrassed cough and began walking, she dropped alongside him matching his pace, he glanced at her, green; her eyes were green, flecked with gold.

"My name is Johnny, John McPhereson."

"Long name."

"John."

"Cam."

"Short name."

She smiled, her face lighting up, lips pulling back from ivory teeth stained with blood. His breath faltered, desire raced through him, not just the usual infatuation, the 10 minute lust, the ogling of cheerleaders and Feed presenters, the glimpse of a breast on the dailies, or furtive surfing on the home-net, imagining the pneumatic models sucking on his cock, letting him fuck them hard, spraying his cum on their boobs as he sprayed his spunk into an old sock. This felt like more, he had never been in love but he knew it would feel like this - the need to have her, to own her, to possess her.

To fuck her.

"What's up?" She said.

He gulped.

"Nothing, we're nearly there."

He indicated his house, glad of the distraction, leant forward to open the gate and stepped back to allow her through, then had to push past her to unlock the front door.

"Kitchens to the left." He said, she looked at him and he shrugged and went first. He opened the cupboard over the fridge and pulled out a large plastic tub with a green cross on it. Cam sat at the breakfast bar, a sheet torn from some kitchen roll dabbed to her lip. She looked around the room, faded, old cabinets, scuffed lino, worn but scrubbed clean. He placed the box in front of her and ripped off the lid, spotting the haemorrhoid cream on the top his face flushed crimson. She smiled at his embarrassment, reached past it for a tube of salve, checked its use by date and dropped it back in.

"It'll heal."

"I can look for some more?"

He was scared now that she'd leave, that would be it, excitement over and no one would believe him in school tomorrow.

"It's fine, I'll have a drink though - you got coffee?"

"Instant."

She pulled a face, mild disgust. "Tea?"

"Yes!"

He jumped up, checked there was water in the kettle and clicked it on to boil.

"Milk, sugar?"

"Neither."

He dropped teabags into a couple of mugs and sat back down. He stared at her, desperate to think of something to say, to appear witty, to make her laugh and see that smile again.

"You want to stop looking at my tits?"

Face flushed, he dropped his gaze, then realised that was probably worse and concentrated on the cupboards behind her head.

"Sorry."

She smiled. "I'm old enough to be your mother."

He couldn't imagine his mum beating up three guys in the street, he couldn't even imagine his dad doing it.

"Who were those guys?" He said.

"They wanted me to go and see a friend of theirs."

"And you didn't want to?"

No need to answer, he could tell from her expression, 'What are you - an idiot?'

"You mind if I smoke?" She said.

"Of course not."

His mother would have a fit. He poured boiling water into

Ten Minus Ten

the cups and mashed the teabags with a spoon, threw them in the bin, added milk and three sugars into one of them. He handed her the other cup.

"Sweet tooth hey?" She said, pulling a battered pack of cigarettes and a lighter from her pocket. He hunted out a souvenir ashtray in the shape of Corfu and placed it on the counter in front of her. She nodded her thanks, flicker of flame crackling the end of her cigarette, she drew the smoke deep into her lungs, exhaled, picked up her cup and sipped tea, wincing from the heat on her cut mouth. She put it back down and sucked on the cigarette, he fixated on her lips, the way they gripped the paper tube, cheeks flattening on the inhale, smoke pluming from her nose on the exhale. She smiled and spoke around it.

"What time your parents get back?"

He glanced at the clock on the wall.

"Half an hour or so."

"Don't worry, I'll be gone by then."

Worry! He didn't want her to go, but what did he want? What he really wanted was to have sex, but realistically he knew that wasn't going to happen. So what did he want?

He gulped some tea, mis-swallowed and tried to mask his choking, not wanting to appear even more of a fool than she already thought him.

She wondered what she was doing there, it had seemed like a good idea to get out of sight, in case any of Marshall's other goons were around, if any of them were more competent than the three who had just attacked her. Getting away from him had been the scariest thing she had done in a while, and now she was stuck in a backwater country with no money and just the clothes on her back. She should have searched those men, but the boy had thrown her off kilter, diverted her from the non plan of just trying to run away as fast as she could. And what about this kid? Always staring at her, kept looking at her tits, going red every other moment, was probably thinking about them fucking. Too young for her, she snatched some cradles but this one was just out of the womb!

She tapped ash, returned the cigarette to her mouth.

"You got any money?" She said.

"What?"

"Money, I don't have any, I need some to catch a bus, or a train or whatever the fuck I need to get out of this place."

"Where do you want to go?"

"The old capital, I've got some contacts there, people who can get me where I want to be."

"That's two hundred miles! I've got some saved but I don't think it'll be enough."

"Enough to get me started?"

"Yes, I guess so."

"Don't worry kid, I'll pay you back."

He bridled at that, at being called a kid and also at being made to look tight, it was just that he didn't have much money, a weekly allowance for tidying his room and putting out the rubbish plus some from his Saturday job. But most of it went on comics and action figures, no way would he tell her that.

"I'll go get it."

"Fine."

He left her and ran upstairs to his room, hastily making the bed and throwing the piles of clothes into a corner. He stopped, what was he thinking? Why was he bothering? Was he going to invite her up? Posters of super heroes, heavy metal bands and scantily clad girls, did he even want her to see his room? He walked to the desk and fished the notes out of a jam jar, scooped up some of the coins scattered about.

Cam smoked the cigarette to the butt, lit another from it, trying to work out her next course of action. Holt used to say 'Getting it is easy, it's keeping it that's hard', caused her to smile again at the thought of him, this had been his country, he'd have known who to contact to get them out, all she had was Greves and he was two hundred miles away with all her money and the morals of a bonobo. She played with her cup and thought of coffee, another reason to get out of this land of weak chinned tea drinkers. Perhaps it was time to go home, take a break, have a holiday, just take it easy on a beach, crashing of the waves, heat from the sun. Fried fish from a hut, cold beer and thick black espresso. What are you doing woman - this isn't the time for daydreaming! She needed to get out of here before Marshall found her, he had misjudged her once and allowed her to escape, she doubted he would be so careless next time, not after the trail of dead she had left in her wake.

She heard footsteps and looked up as the boy came back in. He handed her a few notes, perhaps enough to get her on a train some way to London, dug in his pocket for coins that she waved away.

"This'll do." She said, then thought of the way she was treating him.

"Thank you Johnny."

"John." He wanted her to use a grown up name.

"John." She smiled again, it broadening when she saw the effect it had on him, his face collapsed into desire. "Write down your address, I'll post it back."

"It doesn't matter."

"Don't be foolish."

He coloured and she felt sorry for him, being a teenager sucked, hormones all over the place, desperate to be seen as an adult but lacking the sense and experience to look anything other than a child. She pushed over the cigarette pack, intending for him to write the address on it. He looked puzzled, thinking she was offering him one, should he take it? He'd never smoked, his parents had hammered it into him about the dangers, perhaps he should take one? But what if he choked? That's what they did in Threads when they tried their first one, though they seemed to get over it pretty quickly. Should he be cool, tell her he'd just had one?

"I've given up."

"Write your address." Cam said laughing, the sound making his heart soar while at the same time deepening his crimson flush even further at his mistake. He took a pen from his school bag and wrote it down, not looking at her in case she laughed again.

"Hallloooo." Came from the hall and the front door slammed. Shit, his mum was back! He looked at Cam and tried to stop the panic forming on his face. After all this was perfectly innocent, unfortunately it looked like it would never be anything else. His mother walked in, her smile fading at the scene, a stranger sat at her breakfast bar.

Smoking!

Using her souvenir ashtray!

"Johnny, what's going on?"

"Uh, mum, this is Cam."

"Cam?"

"Yes, she'd been attacked in the street, I offered to help her."

"Attacked! Have you called the police?"

"Your son is exaggerating Mrs McPhereson, it was more of a misunderstanding."

"A misunderstanding?" She glared at this woman, sitting nonchalantly in her kitchen, drinking tea and smoking as if she didn't have a care in the world. And the expression on Johnny's face, like a love sick puppy, he was almost drooling with desire and at a woman who wasn't much younger than herself!

She turned to him. "Johnny, don't you have some homework to do? Ms …?"

She looked at the woman.

"Cam." She supplied, stubbing out her cigarette.

"Cam and I have some grown up things to discuss."

"Mum!"

"You're sixteen!" She shouted more for the woman's benefit than to remind her son.

"Seventeen, I'll be seventeen in a month." He mumbled in reply.

"It's OK John, me and your mum just need to talk."

"Johnny." His mother admonished.

"My, my what a charming domestic scene." Drawled a voice from the kitchen entrance. "So nice to see you in such a setting Cam."

"Marshall." Cam said, he'd found her, she should have run, foolish to relax, what had she been thinking? Sipping tea when she should have been a thousand miles away.

John glared at the man, hate and jealousy flashing through him, was he Cam's boyfriend?

"Who are you?" Shouted his mother "How dare you come into my house?"

She stepped towards him and Marshall raised his hand in a lazy dismissive sweep striking her face with the back of it, knocking her to the floor.

"Mum!" Johnny shouted rushing to her, knelt besides his mother where she lay with her hands over her face.

"Marshall, is there any need for that?"

"Was there any need for killing two of my men and putting another five in hospital?"

"They were in my way."

He shrugged and drew a gun, pushing the barrel against the boy's temple.

"Now are you going to come quietly, or is this going to get messy?"

Fear paralysed Johnny, 'Oh God oh God oh God, I'm going to die!' he thought 'Oh no I'm going to piss myself, please, please, no, not that' The shame of that blocked out the realisation he had a gun to his head, that he was going to die, all he was thinking about was not wetting himself, the embarrassment in front of Cam was more than he could bear.

"Marshall, these people mean nothing to me."

"You won't mind if I kill them then?"

"You don't need the attention of killing citizens, the police will be after you."

"Who do you think owns the police in this town?"

"Still, it's pointless."

"It might be fun."

"Leave them and I'll come with you."

"Ah, now that's better."

He uncocked the gun, tucking it back in his holster.

"Looks like you'll live boy."

Relief swept through John, he was alive and his pants were still dry. He looked down at his mother, staring glassy eyed at her attacker. Cam finished her tea, took the last cigarette from the pack, lit it and pocketed the lighter. Walked round the breakfast bar to Marshall.

"Not so fast." He said, stepping out of the way of the door allowing two of his men into the room.

She looked down at the boy kneeling on the floor, reached out and touched his chin.

"I'm sorry to have got you involved John."

"Cam." He sobbed

"Get out!" His mother screamed.

"Hands." Marshall said and Cam held them out in front of her, handcuffs snapped on by one of the men, the other produced a hood which he pulled over her head, knocking the cigarette to the floor. Lightning fast, Marshall punched her in the stomach, causing her to gasp and double over.

She straightened up and laughed, allowing them to lead her from the house.

Two

Costing him half the cash he had stolen, the taxi dropped him off on Mary the Hopeful. It hadn't been about the money anyway, just something to tie up police resources. A bank robbery had seemed the quickest way to achieve that, but the get-away had been ill thought out, it had almost ended there with his revenge unfulfilled. Stupid to be so careless, Cam would have laughed at his plan, pointed out that surviving was the main priority.

'Do the job once, and do it right'.

Done now, no point dwelling on it, he shifted the rucksack onto his shoulder and walked up the street to the house he had checked out that morning, picked the lock beforehand so that this time he walked straight in, dropped the latch, and went upstairs to the master bedroom. He tipped the rucksack out onto the bed, stripped off his clothes and walked into the en-suite. He squeezed the putty from his nose, balled it up, leaving it on the sink, and got into the shower. Hot water rinsed the dye from his hair colouring the water black as it returned to blond. He flicked the blue contacts free, letting them wash down the drain. Head tilted back, eyes closed, he let himself relax and forget for a moment. As Cam had taught him, he took his feelings and put them aside, he needed to be clear, to follow his plan through without deviation. Pushed down the fear, anger and revulsion at what he had done, crushed it and moulded it like the putty until calm centred him. He dried off and used the towel to wipe out the shower, picked up the putty and went back into the bedroom where he put the towel in the rucksack, the putty in a side pocket. He added his old clothes to it, removed the guns and ammo from the parka and put that in as well. After which he used a can of shredder, spraying it over his body, face and hair and then put on the clothes he had laid out on the bed. A leather jacket covered up the pistol in its shoulder holster and the knife at his belt. He bundled the money, put it and the weapons in the hold-all he had left there. He checked the room, making sure it looked untouched, pausing to watch one of the picture frames scrolling through photos. A happy family on vacation, a couple with their son in between, all grinning, enjoying the trip, abroad by the look of it; the faces of the passers-by were visible behind the three. His parents hadn't taken him out of the county, they had said 'the sea is the sea' and laughed at him paddling in the freezing water dodging the turds and dead fish. Sat in deck chairs drinking cheap wine watching him making castles with oil stained sand. Cold nights in a cheap B&B, sleeping on a fold-down at the foot of their bed, his father's snoring counterpointed by his mother's whistles and grunts. He smiled at the thought, shook his head at his foolishness, left the room and down the stairs, a bag on each shoulder, out through the back, letting the latch drop as he left.

The yard opened out onto shared ground and he wandered the estates rambling paths, making his way down to the shopping parc that sat brooding on the outskirts, boarded and shuttered, only the newsagents still open, mesh protecting it from the drunks and junkies that roamed around it searching through bins and harassing people for change. He pulled out the putty and dropped it down a drain, then handed the rucksack to a beggar. Its contents would be keeping someone warm or in a pawn shop by the end of the day, either way it would be untraceable back to him.

Ten Minus Ten

He pushed open the shop door and walked to the counter.

"Puretones." He said, handing over a twenty, surprised at the lack of change. He had been abroad too long, forgotten how expensive this country was. Leaving the store he paused to light a cigarette, the act making him think of Cam; Puretones, her favourite brand and the only one he had ever smoked. She had taken him and remade him in her image. Her clone she'd said, what she would look like if she had a dick.

He saw his country through her eyes now, the despair and squalor. The dirty, litter covered road, sallow eyed teenagers hanging out on the corners, occasional glances his way, trying to work out if he was an easy take. Grey, overcast sky, always on the edge of rain. She had loved the sun, used to stretch like a cat in it, back arched, her face upturned. She had never wanted to come back here 'Leave Marshall' she had said, but he insisted and now he was alone.

Time for him to move on, standing here was stupid, always move the plan forward, wavering is for wankers. He smiled at the thought, flicked the stub in to the gutter, snatched out by a tramp. But what was his plan? A half formed idea to create trouble for the owners of the Maxi; the super casino on the edge of town. Part of a government scheme to re-energise the city, a private finance initiative where they took all the risk and others took all the rewards. The sharks that ran it used Marshall to keep the locals in check, that was the way to take him down, show them that he couldn't control his patch. Have them step in and step on him. A dangerous game Cam had said, they might just remove Marshall's problem for him, leave him sitting pretty and them dead.

"I want him to suffer, take him down piece by piece, destroy his world, take his life when he has nothing left to lose."

"Too risky." She had said. "If you're going to do it then do it, kill him, revenge over, move on. Instant gratification is what I'm all about." Kissing him deep and hard, making his heart speed as she unbuckled his pants.

He wandered over to the bus stop, the sign telling him that the next one was in five minutes. Cam would be shaking her head, catching a bus, wasn't there a donkey available? It served his purposes, kept him out of sight, allowed him the time to think and besides the police didn't expect bank robbers to take buses.

Another cigarette whilst he waited, he let it fall into the road as the bus pulled in, climbed on saying "The Maxi" to the driver and dropped coins in to the hopper. Ignoring the change he walked halfway down the aisle to an empty seat. His bag next to him and his face turned to the window, watching the streets go past, lost in memories.

He got off two stops before the casino on the road leading up to it, he would walk the remainder, get a lay of the land in the hope that it would give him an idea how to proceed. In the years he had been away nothing much had changed, got a little dirtier, a little seedier but on the whole, the same. He lit a cigarette taking in the scene, mid-afternoon, quiet, most people still at work, a few whores around looking to pick up late lunches, some tramps rooting through rubbish. The pawn and porn shops shuttered but open, dishevelled figures emerging desperate or guilty to shuffle off to the casino or home. This was his country and it was people like Marshall who were destroying it. He would be doing everyone a favour, it wasn't just revenge, he would be making the world a better place.

Lie to everyone else, tell the truth to yourself, if you don't then you'll never know what's fucking real and what isn't. Another Camism, the book of Cam, spoken, beaten, fucked into him.

He was her clone, Cam with a cock, Cam with a conscience.

Conscience, that was never something you could have accused her of. That time in Germany, leaving the man to drown, not worth the effort she had said, don't want to get my shoes wet. And when he had suggested they shoot him she had shrugged, 'he'll drown soon enough, I'm hungry, we'll go eat'.

"You want a good time?" A prostitute approached him, running her hands down her body, pausing on her breasts, her eyes blank and disinterested, sores around her mouth.

"No."

"You gay? You want a man?"

"No."

"Have a bit of fun?"

He sighed, dropped his cigarette and stared into her eyes.

"Fuck off."

She turned away with a muttered. "Fuck you then."

He smiled and lit a new Puretone, started down the street heading in the casino's direction but still not sure what he would do. Walking past one of the cut-throughs he heard cries, the slap of a fist. A woman being beaten by a well dressed man; pimp or angry customer, none of his business either way, she saw him watching and cried out. "Help me, please."

Her face twisting up into an entreaty. He shook his head, not his problem.

"Yeah that's right walk on." Lennon said to the mark, his hand pulled back to deliver another blow. This bitch was always giving him problems, always keeping money back, always pleading for drugs. Fucked up on Grind and any other shit she could get her hands on, still pretty enough to be worth the hassle but she was getting old now and she would have to learn to take what was offered, to blow a tramp if they had the cash and give ninety percent of it to him to pass up the line. He would smack her around a bit more then get her to suck his cock with those bleeding lips. Give her some salt in her wounds, the thought making him grin. He caught sight of the man still lurking at the end of the alley. Maybe he liked watching, maybe he was getting turned on by the sight of her being beaten?

"You want to fuck her? I'll give you a special deal."

"What?"

"You heard, you want to fuck her then it's seventy, otherwise fuck off."

"Don't tell me what to do you fucking cunt." Coming down the alley towards them. Lennon shook his head, what was the fool doing?

"Watch it boy." Lennon said letting go of the girl and stepping forward. "This is Marshall's business, none of yours."

"Marshall?"

"Yes"

"Good."

The man swung his arm out causing Lennon to step back from the expected punch to his jaw, instead a whisper across his throat, a line of pain from the blade cutting his carotid followed by a knee strike that spun him round, crumpling him to the floor. Incomprehension on his face he gripped at his neck feeling the blood spurt through his fingers. He tried to speak, his mumbling unintelligible, vision fading, shook for a few seconds. Went still.

"What the fuck did you just do?" The woman shouted at her rescuer.

"You asked for help." He bent to the corpse and wiped the blade, returned it to its sheath.

"I didn't want you to kill him."

"No, I wanted to kill him."

"Marshall will ... I'm dead, you're dead."

"Fuck Marshall."

He checked the corpse's pockets taking the cash he found, quite a roll, maybe a couple of grand.

"Easier than robbing a bank." He muttered.

"What?"

He stared at her, young, pretty, standard short skirt and

tight top, long black hair, bruised tired eyes. Rucksack on her back in the shape of a rabbit. Bad idea to leave a witness, Cam would have killed her. She could identify him not only to the police but to Marshall's men. The only way she would get out of this alive is if she was of use to them, no guarantee even then.

He peeled off three hundred and handed it to her. "You better run."

"Run to where?"

"Like I give a fuck." He said, walking away leaving her standing staring at the corpse. She was dead, they would never believe her story, they would think she had killed him. Yeah, like if she could have done something like that she would have done it years ago. She looked down at Lennon's body, kicked him hard in the ribs, kicked him again and spat in his face. The fucker, she was dead, why hadn't she just taken the beating? She stuffed the money in to her bag, ran to the end of the alley and looked out, saw the man walking down the street without a care in the world. She was dead, her only way out was giving them the real killer, Marshall might let her go, might just beat her, might let her live. What choice did she have? She wiped the blood from her mouth and followed the man down the road.

He lit a cigarette, felt prickles on the back of his neck, the pressure of someone's gaze that, though irrational, he had been trained not to ignore. He paused to look in a shop window ostensibly admiring the fluorescent dildos instead watching the street's reflection. The girl from the alley, lurking at the corner trying not to be seen. Dressed like a whore was a good disguise in this district but she was too intent on watching him, no interest in the passing trade. Why was she following him? Perhaps to tell Marshall where he went, get a reward or just to stay alive. He cut down a side alley and ducked behind a dumpster, waited for her to follow him in.

"Any reason why I shouldn't kill you?"

She shrieked and backed against the wall. He lit a cigarette, waiting for her answer.

"I...I."

"Yes?"

"I don't have anywhere to go."

"And?"

"I." She shrugged. "I don't know really."

What did she expect of him? That he would look after her? That this was some Portuguese shit where he was responsible for her life now he had saved it? Cam was right, he should have killed her, she always said that he let his emotions get in the way, wasn't prepared to do what needed to be done. She said she loved him for it though. She had said she loved him.

He tapped ash from the cigarette. Maybe the girl could be of use, give him an insight into Marshall's dealings? Or maybe he was looking for a reason not to kill her, not to add her to the list of lives he had taken.

"Your pimp, what was his name?"

"Lennon."

"Like the Beatle?"

"What?"

"Doesn't matter. You know where Lennon took the money?"

"I think so, I followed him once, like I followed you."

"I'm surprised he didn't spot you."

"I was careful."

"You can find it again?"

"Yes." She said staring at him, he was young, early twenties, dark eyes, blond hair, not bad looking.

"You on anything?"

"What?"

"Drugs - you addicted to anything?"

"No, not really, used them but don't need them, why?"

"Cos a junkie isn't to be trusted - they will do anything for their next fix."

"You need to trust me?"

"I would have to trust you if I was taking you with me."

"Take me with you?"

"Show me where Lennon took the money, then we'll talk about it."

He pulled out the cigarette pack and held it out to her, she took one and bent her head to the lighter, cupping her hands around his to shield the flame, she looked up into his eyes, smile tight lipped around the filter hiding her worn down teeth.

"This it then?"

He leant against a wall watching the building on the opposite side of the street, nothing unusual about it except for the heavy stood outside, half shadowed in the recessed doorway but obvious enough.

"Yes, this is where he goes after he finishes his collections."

"Right." He lit a cigarette, absentmindedly holding out the pack to her.

"You know how often Lennon took his in?"

"I don't know, fairly regularly, I followed him once to here, but I don't know how often he did."

He nodded.

"Now you go in there and ask where Lennon is, say he didn't collect his money."

"What? But Lennon's dead!"

"Yes, but you don't know that."

She shook her head, confused. "But I saw you kill him."

"You go in there, say Lennon didn't come and collect his cut this week and you wondered where he was, say you have his money."

He peeled some notes from the roll and handed her them.

"The important thing is that you look around, you count the number of people in there, try and remember the layout, is there a back office or are they all in one room. How are they armed?"

"Armed?"

"What kind of weapons, shotguns, pistols, it doesn't matter about the make, just what they look like."

"I can't do that, they'll kill me."

"You'll just be a whore looking for her pimp."

"I can't, why would I go there?"

"If you're no use to me then I won't protect you."

"Protect me? You're sending me to be killed!"

"You'll be OK if you play it like I said, they'll expect you to be scared, they'll be puzzled why you've come looking for Lennon rather than spending the cash on drugs but they'll think you're too stupid to try it on."

"I can't do this."

"Do you want to be a whore all your life? Dead at thirty?"

"And this is better?"

"I can show you another way."

"Killing people?"

"Robbing them, sometimes killing them, yes."

"That's better than fucking for money?"

"It's easier."

"I don't know."

"What other option do you have? Marshall will kill you, and it won't be a pleasant way to die."

"I could leave, we could leave, we could go to another town, all that money you took from Lennon."

"I'm here to do a job."

"And then?"

"Then I'll leave."

"And you'll take me?"

"If you do this."

She looked down at the money, thought it through, what did she want? Was there more than just her next Grind hit?

"You've given me too much." She handed some back. "They wouldn't believe I would bring that much in."

"So you'll do it?"

"Yes, if you promise to take me with you."

"I will." He looked into her eyes. "Once I am done then we're out of this place."

"OK." She straightened up. "You'll be here when I come out?"

"Yes."

"OK."

She walked out the alley, terrified, feeling like she needed to piss, she crossed the road and over to Marshall's place, stopping in front of the man guarding the door.

He glared at her, made a motioning gesture for her to be on her way.

"I'm looking for Lennon." She said.

"What for?" Carl said, his eyes narrowed in suspicion.

"I've got his money."

"Money?"

"Yes, from you know?"

"Know what?"

"Well, from fucking."

He grunted and indicated for her to hold out her arms so he could perform a body search that lingered on her breasts and slid up the inside of her skirt. Satisfied, he tapped on the glass door to get the attention of the man sat behind a reception desk in the foyer. Bairamov looked at them and made a dismissive gesture, Carl tapped again, pointed at Maya and then at him. Bairamov sighed and buzzed her in.

"What is it?" He said, hands out of sight, she imagined he would be holding a shotgun like they did in the Threads.

"I'm looking for Lennon."

"And you think he's here?"

"I don't know, I just, I'm just, I need to speak to him."

Bairamov pursed his lips, she looked harmless enough,

might be a laugh to send her into the back, puzzle the boys, make them earn their money.

"Go through that door." He said, pointing at the one to his left.

"OK." She pushed it open and went into the office.

She stopped, open mouthed, staring at the sight. Inside there were two desks, the men sat at them sorting cash, loading it into whirring machines that counted and bundled it. Just inside the door was a guard holding a shotgun by the stock. At the back another man stood, a machine gun hanging from a strap over his shoulder.

One of the counters looked up as she entered. "What do you want?"

"I'm." She said, her mouth dry with fear. "I'm looking for Lennon."

"He's not here." Wheeler said.

"I have his money." She walked over to him.

"You shouldn't be here, wait till Lennon comes collecting."

"But, I need."

"Yes?"

"Grind, I need some Grind."

He smiled. "Junkie needs her fix hey?"

"Please."

"Well Yates might be able to help you out, hey Yatesy!"

The man at the back said. "What?"

"Girl here needs some Grind."

"She got any money?" He came over to them, letting his gun swing back on the strap.

She held out the notes she had been given.

"No, money of your own, that's Marshall's, hand it over."

Wheeler took it off her and dropped it on the table. "Doesn't look like she's got any money Yatesy."

"Please." She licked her lips, shifted to push her breasts out.

"Hmm." He pulled out a vial. "Got four shots here, am

willing to treat you guys."

To the other counter he said. "Maeda?" then "Hake?" to the man at the door, received nods and grins from each.

He stared back at her. "How about it, you want four shots for four shots in your mouth?"

She dropped to her knees in front of him and reached for his fly.

Outside she spat in the street, glad to have made it out of there alive and she had some Grind as well! She crossed back over the road and went in to the alley where she had left the man. He wasn't there! She clenched her fists, pressing the nails into her palms, not knowing what to do now. She didn't even know his name! Why would he send her in to that place if he was just going to leave her? There would be easier ways to get rid of her than that.

"How did it go?"

She started, looked round. "Where did you go?"

"I was making sure you weren't followed."

"Checking I hadn't betrayed you?"

"Clever." He lit a cigarette. "Well, they believe you?"

"Yes, I did what you said."

Excited, the rush of adrenaline still coursing through her she began to babble. "There's four of them in a back room."

"Later, later." He wasn't sure if he was disappointed or not, if they had killed her then that was an obligation done with, and now he had to uphold his end of the deal. He held the pack out to her.

"There any hotels near here?"

She accepted a light from him, blew smoke.

"Yes, not far from here, we could walk."

He rolled his arm in a waving gesture.

"Take me to one, we'll talk there."

Minus Nine

Marshall walked into the cell where they held her, closing the door behind him. The custom designed interrogation room he had installed in his basement, walls and floor tiled, with a sluice in the corner, a sink above, its hose attachment coiled around a reel. Glass fronted cabinets displayed an array of surgical and gardening implements. A steel table bolted down in the centre of the room, rings and shackles welded to it, the victims chair similarly fitted out.

They had stripped her naked except for the canvas hood pulled tight over her head, and he gazed at her body, lean and toned, small firm breasts, a tattooed line of words in some foreign language swirled from under the left one down her taut belly and round her hip. He thought of the two times they had fucked, the first, consensual, had been fantastic, she had drained his balls dry. The second, after he caught her stealing from him, had been like fucking a bag of meat, when he came she had looked at him cold eyed and said "Is that it?"

He clenched his fists at the memory. He wanted to throw her to the men, let her be fucked to death, feed her corpse to the pigs. But this was more than revenge this was about money.

He ripped the hood from her head and stared at her face, bloodshot eyes, split lip and broken nose.

"You used to be pretty." He said, his expression a twisted grin, his anticipation of what was to come palpable.

"Still prettier than you." She grinned watching his face change, he was a vain man; easily goaded. One of the reasons she had been able to take his money, he had bragged about his schemes, about how clever he was, how much better he was than other men. She had underestimated the speed with which he would react, the lengths he would go to try and get it back.

He traced a finger down one of the bruises on her arm left by the rubber hoses his men had beaten her with to soften her up in readiness for him, an appetizer before the main course.

"Your tolerance of pain is amazing."

"It's being a woman, childbirth you know and all that shit. Men are weak little pussies, run crying to their mommies."

He smiled at that. "It will be hard to break you."

"Better let me go then, and we'll call it quits."

"I want my money back."

"Sorry, spent it."

"You've spent it?"

"Yeah, I bought one of those fancy cappuccinos, the ones they serve cold."

He gripped her arm, pressed his thumb in to the crook of her elbow.

"You trying to be funny?"

"They cost more than you think."

"Where is my money?"

"How much was it again?"

"Ten million pounds."

She nodded. "What's that in dollars, a couple of bucks?"

He slapped her open handed across the face spraying blood.

"Don't get tetchy." She said. "I meant Michigan dollars."

His hand arced back the other way, crunching into her nose.

"Going to be tricky to set." She sniffed. "Might end up with one like yours."

He touched his face, feeling the proud straight nose that had cost him several thousand to be happy with, was tempted to hit her again but this wasn't getting him anywhere. He marvelled at her reaction, she didn't even seem to register the pain.

"I think we'll need to get a bit more inventive."

"You could be in trouble then." She said.

"What?"

"Well it's not your strong point is it? Original thinking I mean."

"You bitch!"

He punched her, snapping her head back, raised his fist, changed his mind and walked over to the door, wrenched it open, shouted out in to the hallway.

"Stoker, get in here!"

Hearing footsteps outside he moved to one side, his hands on his hips. She ran her tongue around the inside of her mouth, pushed a tooth feeling it wobble, spat, the saliva dribbling down her chin.

Nigel Stoker came in to the room, his eyes alive at the prospect of witnessing someone suffering.

"Mr Marshall?"

"Fasten her hand, the left one."

Stoker unshackled her arm, she twisted it free and tried to gouge his eyes, he wrestled with her, needing all his strength to restrain her, managed to drag her hand to the table and push her fingers through the rings welded to its surface, splaying them out. He clamped her wrist and stepped back.

"Done Mr Marshall."

"Took your time."

He opened a cabinet and took out a pair of bolt cutters.

"Let's see how lippy you are after I chop a few fingers off."

He held them in front of her face, opened the blades and slid it over her little finger, closed them until it began to bite in to the flesh.

"I'm going to slit you from throat to belly and then cut off your cock and watch you choke to death on it." She said, preparing herself for the pain, building her anger to get the adrenaline flowing.

"Bit hard without fingers." He tightened their grip slicing her skin, blood oozing from the cut.

"I'm pretty resourceful."

"We'll see" He snapped them closed, snipping through the flesh and bone, her finger dropping free.

She hissed once, then was silent, he was amazed, how could she ignore that?

He put the cutters down and picked up the digit.

"I'll keep this as a souvenir."

"And I'll take one of your balls."

"Give me my money and I'll let you go."

"You got a cigarette?"

"Sure."

He took one out and placed it in her mouth, crushed and bruised lips he wanted to kiss, to bite, pull from her face. When he had his money he would take his time, make her pay, make her regret stealing from him, make her beg for him to kill her.

He lit the cigarette and stepped back.

"My money?"

She drew on it, pulling the smoke deep into her lungs, trying to keep a handle on the pain, her techniques beginning to crumble under this onslaught, they were intended for battlefield trauma, to keep it at bay for a short time until you could get treatment, not for this. She nodded at the blood pulsing from her finger.

"Can you sort that out?"

"Oh. I'm sorry." He grabbed the cigarette from her mouth and pressed the burning tip against the wound.

She hissed again, then pushed the pain away, looked him steadily in the eyes and said

"You got a cigarette?"

Three

The hotel she took him to was several streets from the place where Marshall's money was counted. They had walked in silence, stopping once to buy more cigarettes and a couple of stale looking sandwiches, the bread curling up at the edges in a vain attempt to get away from the dubious filling. He had eaten half of his and thrown the rest away, she had left hers in the plastic wrapping, tucked it in to the top of her bunny bag. She found it hard to keep to his pace, shoes designed to show off her calves were no use for the forced march she was subjected to and she was now beginning to reconsider her choices.

"Why do you want a hotel anyway?" She said.

"What's the usual reason people want a hotel?" He spoke around a cigarette, the end bobbing with his words.

"I don't know." She shrugged. "To fuck?"

Surprise on his face. "You think I'm taking you to a hotel to fuck you?"

"Well, why else?"

"I need to rest, plan."

"Plan?"

"Yes."

She waited for him to continue, frowned when he said nothing.

"Plan?" She said.

"Yes."

She scowled, kicked a stone watched it ricochet off a lamppost.

"Good shot."

"What? Oh, that." Decided not to tell him it was an accident.

"You use the hotels a lot?"

"What? You mean to fuck, no, not really."

This was an area of industrial estates and cheap motels with large car parks, ideal for the road warrior and other itinerants. Girls hung around the streets, easy to pick up a client here and they could work out of a room for a fifteen percent cut to the management. Maya's usual patch was closer to the centre, she worked the punters on their way to and from the casino, most of the time in their cars or down a side alley like the one where Lennon had beaten her.

Where Lennon had been killed.

By this man.

Would he kill her? Once she had told him about Marshall's place she was of no further use to him. Just a witness, someone to tie him to Lennon's murder. Should she run? She had some Grind and the money he had given her. She could get on a bus, get away from here, to the next town at least, and then what? Was his offer better? What did it even mean? He said he would teach her how to rob and kill, how was that any nobler than selling your body? At least what she did didn't harm anyone.

Except herself.

But she didn't deserve any better did she? Her mother had always told her she was useless, a mistake coming off Fen because her boyfriend had wanted kids and then he dies before she's born. Not paying attention when he crossed the road, too busy staring at the scan of his child on his Perse. Too late to abort, just a millstone around her neck, well she could pay her way now couldn't she? This nice man is going to give us some money, go with him and do as you're told. Be useful for a change.

She was sick of being used, now she would take it back.

Decided she straightened her back, stumbled and grabbed for him. He steadied her, his touch on her arm firm but gentle. He waited for her to regain her balance before letting go.

"Thank you." She said.

He ignored the comment. "You recommend any?" He nodded at the row of motels.

"They all charge the same."

"That one then." He said, walking over to the nearest.

It was run down, decrepit, the shrubbery overgrown and unkempt, a path to the front entrance appearing more accidental than deliberate. The sign flickered in the afternoon sun advertising cheap rates and air con. She raised an eyebrow as he held the door for her, he scowled and ushered her through. Inside the fluorescents did little to lift the gloom, the filthy window not letting in much light, making the yellow walls look brown. The carpet tiles worn and mismatched, their pattern disrupted by efforts to increase their life span through rotation. There was an overriding smell of strong bleach. Opposite the door was a hole cut in to the wall giving access to a small office in which sat the receptionist. Above was a ticker giving the prices in hours and a list of house rules.

He tapped on the lopsided shelf that served as a counter, received a grunt of acknowledgement, the man refusing to look up from his Perse.

"I need a room."

"How long for?" His eyes on an entertainment feed, latest gossip on Thorsten or one of the other CellEnts.

"Five hours."

"Hmm?" The sound betraying interest and the man looked up at him, eyes alight with curiosity, wondering what he had in mind for a whore that would take that long.

"Five hours."

"Seventy, plus ten key deposit, you want towels, that's

another ten."

He handed over ninety, received a room key and a plastic bag with a couple of threadbare towels in it.

"End of the corridor, room 156."

"OK." He walked away, not waiting to see if she followed him.

He opened the door to the room, ushered her in then locked it behind them, rummaged in his bag and pulled out a black rectangle of shiny plastic, one side dimpled with holes, the opposite spiked. He pressed it on to the frame.

"What's that?" She said.

"A screamer - if the door's opened it will go off, you don't want to experience it."

"What if I want to go out?"

"You don't, unless you ask me."

"Am I a prisoner?"

"For the moment, yes, pretty much."

She nodded and looked round the room, the usual hour stop, marked walls, a dilapidated bed, a scuffed table with a single chair pushed under it. She took off her furry rabbit rucksack and hung it on the back.

"Doesn't that put them off, your, um, clients?" He said.

"No, they like it, makes them feel like they're fucking their daughters."

Face still he processed her words.

"Right." He said after a moment.

"You never told me your name." She said.

"No, I didn't."

"Mine's Maya."

"Oh."

"And?"

"And?"

"What's yours?"

"It's irrelevant."

"Funny name."

He laughed.

"I have to call you something." She said.

Thinking he squinted, made up his mind and said.

"Call me Chris."

"Chris?"

"Yes."

"Chris, can I get a shower?"

"OK."

She peeled her top over her head revealing pert young breasts, he blinked, colour rising in his cheeks and turned his head away.

"What's the matter?" She unzipped her skirt and let it drop to the floor.

"Nothing."

Staring at the wall, uncomfortable with her nudity, embarrassed at his response to it, a man who killed without thought blushing at the sight of a prostitute. But other than teenage fumblings, his experience was limited to Cam. He was aroused and it felt like a betrayal, Cam wouldn't have cared, she would laugh to see him like this.

Maya was puzzled by his reaction, she had lost count of the men who had seen her naked, though the majority of times she had just pulled up her skirt - a quick rut in an alley or a blowie, spunk spat into the gutter. The first time had been different, the rich man who had paid to take her virginity. An expensive hotel; a Travel Lodge on the edge of town. It had complementary towels, one stained with her blood taken as a memento.

"Are you gay?" She said.

"No."

"Then why aren't you looking at me?"

"Just giving you some privacy."

She laughed, took the plastic bag from him and walked into

the bathroom, he could hear taps turning and the sound of water. Cursing he burst in. Shocked, she shielded herself with a towel, dropped it and moved her legs apart.

"You want to fuck me?"

He blushed again, mumbled. "I needed to check if there was a window."

"In case I tried to escape?"

"Yes."

Well, there isn't." She pointed to the extractor. "Don't think I can squeeze through that."

"No."

"So you want to fuck me then?"

He turned without saying anything, pulled the door closed behind him.

She stepped into the shower, wishing there was a tub instead, a long soak would help with the withdrawal, four shots, she had four shots. Four shots and then what? She put her head under the spray, feeling the dirt washing from her hair and face, the heat soothing, helping her to forget for a moment.

He paced the room, frustrated, this felt like a waste of time, a pointless deviation from his mission.

Mission, ha!

He laid on the bed, trying to think through what was to come next, his plan half formed, not even that. This venture had cost too much already, he should cut his losses and leave now. He should have listened to Cam, she had told him there was no satisfaction from revenge. She had warned him and it had been her who paid the price.

And now he was alone.

Except there was the girl, Maya. Why had he agreed to take her with him? She was a distraction, he should have dealt with her in the alley, she would get in his way, get him killed. He wiped the tears from his face and took the pistol out of his shoulder holster. He would need to get a suppressor from his bag, or he could just use a pillow.

Maya came out of the bathroom, naked except for the towel wrapped round her hair.

"Feels good to be clean again." She said, her smile faltering at the sight of the gun.

Cam used to wrap her hair in a towel turban whilst it dried, a cigarette hanging from her lips. She would sit watching him field strip his automatic, teasing him for his obsession with guns. Made him stop to rub moisturiser into her skin, cursed at him for getting gun oil on her, laughed at his grumbling reply.

The pistol down by his side he stared at her, undecided.

"Chris?"

He re-holstered it, pointed at her rucksack.

"You got any clothes in there, ones that don't make you look like a whore?"

"But I am a whore."

"How old are you?"

"Sixteen."

"How long have you been doing this?"

"Since I was twelve."

Christ and he thought his childhood had been taken away.

He pointed at his bag. "There's some clothes in there, might be a bit big but…"

"OK."

She squatted and rummaged through it pulling out a machine pistol, he crossed the floor and snatched it from her, took the bag as well and emptied it onto the bed. She gawked at the bundles of cash that spilled onto the duvet. He pushed them aside, sorting through the clothes, picking out a sweatshirt and a pair of jeans which he threw at her.

"They're too large." She said holding them up against herself, thinking about all that money on the bed, wondering how she could get hold of it.

"They'll do for the moment."

She shrugged and pulled on the jeans, she twisted the waistband to hold them up.

"Got a belt?"

He picked up a coil of rope, cut a length off and threw it to her. She threaded it through the loops and tied at the front, bent to roll up the trouser legs. The sweatshirt swamped her, coming almost to her knees.

"I look like a kid in this."

"You are a kid."

"You're not much older."

"Yeah, I guess not."

"Now what?"

"I need to get some sleep, do I need to tie you up?"

"Why?"

"Will you try and kill me?"

"I, I, no, I wouldn't."

"Didn't say you would, said you might try. Get on the bed, the wall side."

She climbed on and lay down, her arms by her sides, nervous, unsure what he had in mind, this was worse than being with a punter, at least then you knew what was going to happen, but he, what would he do to her? He had a gun in his hand when she came out of the bathroom. He had looked like he was going to kill her. She should have wrapped the towel around her body, played it coy, he was shy, she could have seduced him, made him want her, made him need her. He was going to kill her, she had seen it in his eyes, he had changed his mind, but what would stop him changing it again?

He got on to the bed next to her, turned his head and said. "Don't get up until I wake up, sleep if you can, keep still if you can't."

He looked up at the ceiling, shifted to get comfortable and shut his eyes.

"How long will you sleep?" She said.

"Two hours."

"Two hours exactly?"

"Near enough."

"Wow, how do you do that?"

"Shut up."

He closed his eyes. Maya watched him for a while, wondered what to do, he expected her to lie there, just lie there? The Grinddown was coming on and she had four hits in her bag. She sighed, better deal with the now. She eased herself down the bed to the end trying to be quiet, went to the table and opened the back pocket of her bag. Palmed a shot and headed for the bathroom.

"Where are you going?"

Sat up, staring at her, Christ this was a bad idea, he needed to focus on the task in hand, not get caught up babysitting.

"The toilet, you know, for."

"Ah, right."

He coloured, waved her on and closed his eyes.

She shut the door behind her and breathed out, luckily he hadn't questioned her, she could hardly have said she was going to do some Grind, he had been fairly emphatic on how he felt about junkies.

She popped the pellet into her mouth and bit lightly on it, grinding some away, dissolving it in her spit, not too much at once, newbie mistake to crunch down, one huge orgasm followed by intense despair, better to let it build, teeth working slowly, pleasure rising and washing over her, mouth going like a cow, eyes rolling up, feeling it now, stifling a yelp she dropped to her knees, shudder through her body, this is what she had imagined sex was like when she had giggled about it with her friends at school. Before the reality when that man took her cherry, hard thrusts and pain, nothing more than fear and the wooze of too much drink. The times after no better, only Grind, meth and dope kept her alive, gave her hope for more than this, more than to be fucked for money, violated on camera, pissed and spat upon, bound and beaten then thrown back on to the street, only the drink and drugs kept her numb enough not to care, to stop her from slitting her wrists or jumping into a canal. Only the hope that this wasn't all there was, and the sweet feeling of Grind as she passed out on the floor.

Minus Eight

"What have you got to say for yourself!?"

Dennis McPhereson paced back and forth in front of his son, hands alternating between clenched fists and waving around. Pressed back in to the sitting room sofa John tried to answer, his words cut off with a gesture from his father.

"You bring a strange woman into this house, and when one of her friends turns up he assaults your mother!"

Dennis pointed at his wife sat in the chair by the Ent, her eyes red and puffy from crying, an ugly bruise on her cheek.

"I don't think he was her friend." John said.

"What sort of excuse is that?"

"She'd been attacked! I was only trying to help!"

Coming home from a shift at the Centre, eight hours of being lied to by claimants, being cajoled and pleaded with, threatened and abused and all he had wanted was to sit down in front of the Ent with a beer. Instead this; Sheila assaulted by a man with a gun, in their own home! This wasn't a Thread, it didn't happen in real life.

"Did she need your help?"

John thought about Cam standing there, having punched that guy, kicked the other one. Panting, out of breath but victorious, she hadn't looked like she'd needed any assistance.

"She was hurt." He said.

"Look at your mother!"

John stared at his mother sniffling into a tissue, knew he

was supposed to feel upset, to be sorry for the pain she was in, but all he could feel was contempt. Cam wouldn't have cried, she spat blood and struck back.

"Mum, I'm sorry." His words empty and devoid of feeling.

"That's it?"

John looked up at his father, shrank back from the rage and hate showing on his face, he held his hands up, waited for the blow. His dad stood in front of him, his shoulders hunched up, arms by his sides, fists clenched. A desire to strike his son, to teach him a lesson, welling up inside. To do something rather than this feeling of impotence.

"That's all you have to say?"

"Den, leave it now." Sheila said. She blew her nose, crumpled the tissue and tucked it in to her sleeve, pushed her hair back from her face and straightened up.

"Johnny, go to your room." She said.

John looked from one to the other, shuffled along the sofa to be out of his dad's reach before standing. He left the room, shutting the door on the start of an argument, their voices fading as he climbed the stairs.

In his bedroom he grabbed his Perse off the desk and dropped on to his bed, plugged the buds into his ears and closed his eyes. They were being so unreasonable, he hadn't wanted his mother to get hurt, how could he have known that someone would march into their house uninvited? They didn't even seem to care that Cam had saved his life, she could have fought her way out, he had no doubt about that, probably have killed the man with the ashtray or her cup of tea!

Yeah, she could have flung the cup in his face scalding him, then taken the gun and... but instead she had gone with them, let herself be taken to protect him.

He sat up, he had to do something to help her, at least tell the police. But that man, Marshall, said he owned the cops, no help there, more likely be putting himself at risk as well. He looked at the poster on the wall opposite his bed, the Justifier surrounded by enemies, grim determination on his face, surrender not an option.

He could save her himself, find out where they had taken her, sneak in and free her. She'd be so grateful she might even let him kiss her.

Decided, he rolled off the bed jumping to his feet, hands held in an attack pose. Threw wild punches and kicks, caught his foot on the wardrobe door and fell on his arse. He lay on the carpet, listening for a shout from downstairs. He got back to his feet and opened the window, his plan being to climb down onto the extension's flat roof and then a short drop to the ground. He sat on the windowsill, hands gripping the ledge, looking down at the drop, changed his mind and twisted round on to his stomach, his legs dangling, toes pressing against the brickwork. Once he was down he would get a bus to...

Money!

He would need some to get into town and he had given all of his to her, the few coins remaining not enough for the bus journey. He scrabbled up, dropping head first back in to his room, stood up and brushed at the dirt on his sweatshirt.

He opened his bedroom door, stepping out into the hall and down the stairs, treading lightly and sticking to the edge to minimize creaks. He paused in front of the living room door, it was quiet inside, his parents watching a comedy or documentary. Both paying little attention, his dad feeling useless, his mother afraid. He walked past into the kitchen, his mother's handbag lay on the table, he opened it and took the cash out of her purse, thought for a moment and then removed a credit card as well. Cam could use it to buy a train ticket to London.

If he could find her.

Taking his coat from the rack, he eased the front door open, left the house, pulling it shut behind him. Stood for a few seconds in the cool night air trying to figure out what he was going to do next. To find Cam he had to find Marshall, he was the one who had her. If she was alive. But she must be. It hadn't looked like he was going to kill her, well not straight away. So he had to find Marshall, find out where he lived, or where he would take her.

Down-town was the obvious choice, where the thieves, junkies and whores hung out. This Marshall was a criminal, if anyone knew where he was it was other lowlifes. How could he persuade them though? What would they do in a Thread? Beat someone up, talk to a grass. He didn't know any snitches, and as for beating someone up...the only fight he had been in was against Tanya Riley and that hadn't ended well. This whole idea was beginning to feel stupid, maybe he should just go back in, forget about the whole thing? He hesitated, unsure what to do, but at least he could try, not live with the regret that he should have done something. He jogged down the path and vaulted the gate, ducked down past his fence, hand ready to draw his imaginary gun, headed for the bus stop at the end of the street.

The numbers on the shelter's screen counted down to zero and two minutes later the bus pulled alongside. John got on, showing his pass and dropping coins into the hopper. He took a seat halfway down, staring out the window avoiding the other passengers eyes. They meandered around the city, office workers getting off in the suburbs as the tired and the forgotten got on for the trip to the casino and another night of shattered dreams.

He rang the bell on St. Jacqueline the Giving, the main road leading to the super casino. The street was lined with apartment blocks, the ground floors given over to shops that the developers had intended to be wine bars and delicatessens but in reality had become off-licences and pawn brokers. Stepping off, he zipped his coat up to the collar and looked at the gloomy street. Broken lights, rubbish piling up in the dark alleys and doorways, people lurking in the half shadows. Unsure what he was going to do he started off up towards the casino, keeping near the road, hunched up, trying not to look a threat.

A prostitute approached him. "You looking for some action Honey?"

He paused a second, not knowing what to say, what to ask. She stood waiting for an answer, a hand on her hip, one foot beginning to tap. He considered turning, just walking away, this was stupid, what was he doing?

Surprised himself by blurting.

"I'm looking for a man called Marshall."

"Marshall? He doesn't swing that way, likes pussy that one."

"Please, I just need to find him."

She looked at him, this skinny kid that shouldn't be out here, should be at home playing Rubads with the folks or some such shit. He was trembling, whether from the cold or scared it didn't matter, not after a fuck so he was wasting her time.

"Finding Marshall isn't to be recommended." She said.

"Please."

"I'm doing you a favour." She said and walked away.

He watched her, ashamed at how he had handled the conversation, at not knowing what to say. A woman had been listening to them, she came over and put her hand on his arm, her eyes unfocused, smile showing yellow teeth.

"For ten pounds I'll tell you where Marshall lives, for thirty I'll throw in a hand job, fifty and I'll suck your dick, and for eighty you can stick it in my tight juicy wet hole, make you a man, how about it?"

Embarrassed he mumbled. "Just the ten."

She laughed. "Give me it."

He fumbled in his pocket and pulled out a note, checked its value and handed it over. She smoothed it out and tucked it in the waistband of her skirt.

"You're in the wrong part of town, Marshall lives up in Elysium Delights, you know the big houses behind the gates?"

"He lives in E.D.?"

"Yeah, you think a man with that much money is going to live round here? You even know who he is?"

"Not really, he took a friend of mine, I'm going to get her back."

"Well that friend of yours is dead, and you will be too if you go up there."

"Please, just tell me which his house is."

"The highest one on the hill, looking down on all the others, that motherfucker owns this town, owns us all, decides if we live or die. You should stay away if you want to keep breathing."

"Thank you." He began walking back to the bus stop. Watching him go she called after him.

"You sure you don't want to fuck? I'll do you for seventy, you don't want to die a virgin."

"Thank you, no." Ignored the laughter that followed him down the street.

The bus route terminated at Boniface the Repentant, people who lived in Elysium Delights had no use for public transport, and those that serviced their needs; cooks, cleaners etc. were picked up each day by minibus if they weren't fortunate to be quartered there. A few people got on at the Boniface stop but he was the only one to disembark at that time of night. It was getting dark, the street-lights coming on as he passed them on the way to the gated community at the top of the hill.

The entrance had an automatic barrier monitored by a guard hut, its door closed, light flickering from inside, reflected on the window. He walked past it following the wall looking for a way in. Two metres high and topped with cutters, impossible to climb over. He doubled back and approached the hut, crept up to the window and glanced in at the Rentacop sat on a folding chair, legs propped up on a desk, watching a Thread on his Perse. He crouch walked past, ducking under the bar and edged round, holding his breath, stood up at the other side, tense, waiting for the shout. He ran up into the estate, slowing when he realised he might look suspicious. The houses he passed were all detached with large gardens, expensive cars parked on their drives, he kept his head down trying to be inconspicuous, just a kid on his way home, he walked up the hill to the building at its apex.

This one also had its own wall, more for show it looked climbable, rough stone, plenty of handholds with a scrolled ironwork gate closing off its drive from the rest of the estate. They had been built in its grounds, newer, no more than 50 years old whilst this one must have been in its hundreds, looming grand and imposing over them. John walked alongside the wall until he felt he was far enough away from the entrance to be seen and scrabbled up it, jamming his toes into the gaps and pulling himself up onto the top before lowering down the other side. He crouched looking up at the house, mustered his courage and ran across the lawn to it. How was he going to get in? Close up the windows were sealed shut, trip alarms obvious, the doors would be the same.

He could just knock.

And say what? "I've come for Cam."

Marshall had pulled out a gun in their home, he would have no problem doing it here, except maybe for the noise, probably have a silencer. Or have his henchmen cart him off and dispose of him somewhere more private. This was stupid, why had he come? He was just a kid, he couldn't help her. There was no guarantee that she was in there, this might all be for nothing, just get into more trouble, more grief from his folks.

He should go home.

Ten Minus Ten

He walked round the building, ducking under windows, looking for an easy way in. Nothing, he shouldn't have expected anything less from a crime lord. His feet clattered on something and he looked down, a manhole cover, no, a coal chute. He had read about them in history, burning fossil fuels to heat your home, delivered by horse and cart! He felt round the edge, fingers hunting for purchase, pushed them into a gap, grunting, he managed to lift it slightly, got his hands under it and slid it to one side. He could get in this way, into the coal cellar, if it still led there, if it wasn't blocked off, a dead end. It looked quite narrow, a tight squeeze even for him. He took his coat off dropping it on to the cover and sat down on the edge with his feet dangling, pushed forwards, sliding in, fingers keeping a grip on the rim. He hung, still unsure if this was a good idea. Good idea, who was he kidding? He was breaking into a house! His arms began to ache from the weight, the metal cutting in to his flesh. Limbs trembling from the strain, it was a relief to let go. A short slide followed by a fall in to darkness, a jarring shock when he hit the floor, twisting his ankle in the process.

Winded, his cry was little more than a gasping moan. He lay trying to get his breath back, at last able to sit up he pulled his Perse out and keyed the display, the blue light turning the darkness into gloom. He was in a small room, some boxes scattered about, no coal that he could see, the chute stuck out of the wall above his head and at the other end there was a door. He rubbed his ankle reluctant to put any weight on it, waited for the pain to lessen before he tried to stand. Seemed OK, he limped over to the exit and eased it open a fraction looking through the gap at a brightly lit corridor, white walls and tiled floor, stairs off to the left, a way up into the house?

There were other doors, one opposite his, another further along which opened and he heard a man say. "We'll leave you to think about it."

He quietly pushed his shut, listened to footsteps walking past.

'Leave you to think about it?' Could he have been talking to Cam? It sounded like Marshall, it would make sense to keep her down here. He opened the door again and looked out, no one around, he stepped in to the hallway and approached the one they had come out of.

Tiled like the corridor, glass fronted cabinets on the walls, a table in the centre with a chair on either side.

A woman, her head covered by a canvas hood, sat on one of them.

A naked woman.

Bruises all over her body, her naked body.

A tattoo snaked from her perfect breasts down to round her hip.

His cock was getting hard, he felt confused about his reaction. She was beaten, hurt, but he was turned on by the sight of her, he didn't know what he had walked into, what was going on here. There was blood on the table, some dripping on the floor.

"Forgot something you cunt?"

"Cam?"

The hood tilted towards him. "Who the fuck are you?"

"It's me Cam, John."

He pulled it from her head. Confused, she stared at him, it was the boy from earlier, the house where she had been recaptured.

"What the fuck are you doing here? Does Marshall think you can persuade me? I'm sorry kid but you're just going to get killed."

"I've come to rescue you!"

"Yeah, right." She laughed. "Where's Marshall? What's this game he's playing? If you think I care about this kid Marshall."

The final words said louder to those she imagined were

standing outside the room.

John's face fell, hopes of being a hero crushed. She called him a kid again, laughed at the idea of him rescuing her. He examined the restraints on her hands, gasping as he saw the wound where her little finger had been.

"Are you all right?"

"Am I all right? Those motherfuckers beat me with hoses and cut off a finger, sure I'm all right."

"Beat you? Cut off your finger?" He paled, felt sick.

"John, undo these." She rattled her wrists and he saw that they were fastened with a wing-nut, the bar between preventing the captive from undoing it themselves.

"Oh, right, sure." He spun them loose freeing her hands.

She bent down and unshackled her feet, even if this was a trick she would be better off if she could kick a few heads in, the kid wasn't going to slow her down. This time she would fight to the death before she let them tie her to that chair again.

"See if there's anything medical in those cupboards." She said.

He went over to the closest cabinet and opened it. Inside were hammers, pliers, all sorts of tools which he realised, with a sickening feeling, were used on people, to torture them, to torture Cam. He turned to her, trying not to vomit.

"Anything in there?"

"Uh." He swallowed, checked the others, found bandages and a can of antiseptic. He held them out to her.

"Looks like he doesn't want his victims to die too quickly." She said taking them off him with a smile.

She squirted the spray onto her stump and then wound the bandage around it, holding the ends towards him she said. "Tie a knot."

"Uh, OK." He fumbled one, blushing at the touch of her.

"Look John, if we get out of here then we'll fuck, but keep your mind on the game until then right?"

"Uh." He stammered, not knowing how to reply.

"How did you get in here?"

"There's a coal cellar, a coal chute, I came down that."

"A coal chute?"

"They used to deliver coal, wagon pulled by horses, they drop the coal down the chute and you used it to heat your house."

"I see."

"We did it in history."

"History, right. Show me this coal chute."

"OK."

She went to the door, expecting Marshall to be stood there laughing at his joke. But at least her hands were free, she could do some damage. She wouldn't let them use the kid against her, snap his neck if this was a ruse, be doing him a favour, they wouldn't let him live after this. He followed her, eyes focused on her arse. It was as good as he had imagined. The line of words curved round her waist ornate and indecipherable.

"What do they say?"

"Huh?" Distracted she looked back at him.

"The words, your tattoo."

"Life song."

"Really?"

"Yes, I'm hoping it will reach down my leg."

"What's it say?"

"We don't have time for this, which way is this coal chute?"

"Oh yeah, down here."

He cut in front of her to lead the way, head darting about, listening for guards, his heart beating fast, the sight of Cam, the injuries she had suffered, it made it all real, this wasn't a game, if they were caught he could expect the same, worse as they didn't want anything from him. He would just be their toy, the realisation of what he had done, what he was doing caused him to stop, Cam almost bumping into him.

"What is it?" She asked, thinking he had heard something, getting ready to kill she shifted on to the balls of her feet.

"Sorry, nothing."

He opened the door to the coal cellar, closing it behind them and used his Perse to provide light. She looked around, some boxes piled up, not any coal that she could see, if she knew what the fuck coal looked like. He pointed at a hole in the far wall, she went and inspected it.

"You've got to be fucking kidding."

"It's quite short, maybe a couple of metres."

"I don't think I'll fit."

"It's not too bad."

"For you maybe."

"I'll push you."

"You'll push me? I told you we would fuck, you don't have to try and cop a feel."

Fear was beginning to overwhelm him, that room, those implements for torturing people. To torture him if they were caught. All he wanted to do now was get out, to be safe back at home, all this behind him.

He lost his temper. "Look just get up there!"

Cam smiled. "That's better, show some balls."

She pushed a box under the chute and climbed up into it, putting her arms forward trying to get a purchase on the inner walls. She pushed them apart, gripping by friction, her legs scrabbling as she moved up the tunnel. If Marshall was waiting at the top then she was fucked, but that was no reason not to try. Sometimes you just have to do, the fear of what might happen can cripple you, paralyse you in the now.

He watched her disappear, his cock painfully hard as her arse slid out of view. He wouldn't be able to get out now, he wouldn't be able to walk let alone climb up, he would get it caught on the edge like the barb of a fishing hook. He would have to wait until it subsided, or perhaps he should have a wank? He giggled, what if he got caught jacking off? Marshall and his men walking in and finding him with his trousers round his ankles.

They would chop it off, use some of the tools hanging in the cabinets. The fear washed over him, instantly limp, well at least that was one problem dealt with and when he got out she said they could fuck.

His cock twitched back into life.

"Oh no, no, no, no."

At the top Cam gripped the edge of the chute, pulled up and rolled out on to the grass, glanced around looking for Marshall and his men. Nothing, quiet. She listened for sound from the boy, nothing, she stuck her head back in and whispered a question.

"I'm coming." He gasped, creeping up the pipe, this far harder than sliding down, exhaustion beginning to set in, the pain of pushing against the edges with his arms, his feet scrabbling for purchase. He reached out and felt her grab and pull him up, surprised at her strength, she dragged him out, letting go as he cleared the edge.

"Thanks." He said.

She crouched. "So what's the next stage of your plan?"

He lay on his back, trying to get his breath, trying to control his fear. She loomed over him, her face centimetres from his.

"John, focus, what now?"

"There's a guard post at the bottom of the hill, the guy inside is watching a Thread, we should be able to sneak past." He sat up and peeled off his sweatshirt "Here you can wear this"

She took it with a muttered thanks, pulling it on she stood up.

"Let's leave before Marshall comes back." She said.

He nodded and grabbed his coat, holding it out to her, she shook her head, he shrugged and put it on.

"There's a wall but it's easy, then we're in the main community, short walk to the guard post, it's just a barrier, we should be able to sneak past."

"Let's get on with it then."

Infuriated he turned and headed for the wall. She followed him, still unsure if this was a trick, waiting for the shout, Marshall's sardonic laughter, the click of a trigger cocking.

John, angry and scared, scrambled up the wall and dropped down the other side, crouched waiting for her to follow. She landed beside him, rose up in one smooth motion.

"OK?" She said.

"OK." He stood up.

She could tell he was going to crack, she had seen it before, you can drive someone so far, scare them so much and then they were useless, she needed him, at least for a little while longer.

"John." She stepped closer and wrapped her arms around him. "Thank you."

He relaxed into her embrace as she hugged him tighter, smiling at the pressure of his erection on her stomach.

Releasing him she said. "Shall we get out of here?"

"Um, yes."

He dropped his arms, one over his crotch. "The guard post is that way." He said, pointing back down the hill.

He approached the barrier first, a quick peek, beckoned her to follow and snuck under the bar, waiting for her on the other side. She moved silently, pausing beneath the window, debating whether to go in, kill the guard and get his gun. She looked over to John waving frantically at her, sighed and carried on.

"What is it?" She said.

"I thought you might get caught."

"I'm touched, now what?"

"Down the hill - there's a bus stop, we'll get one into town."

"A fucking bus! We're going to wait for a bus? I'm half naked! Don't you think that will raise suspicions?"

He looked at her, the sweatshirt came to mid thigh, no more indecent than what most girls wore for a night out, nothing out of the ordinary, except, maybe, the lack of shoes.

"Well what do you suggest?"

"A car?"

"I can't drive."

She rolled her eyes. "Forget it, let's go to the bus stop, I need to get a train out of here."

"There's a bus to the interchange, I checked the times, there's a train to London every two hours, but ..."

"But?"

"Nothing." No opportunity to have sex if she got on a train.

"OK, lead on."

Despondent he led her to the stop. The pair waited in silence for the bus to pull up. Boarding, John said. "Two for St Augustus." and paid. She gave him a puzzled glance which he ignored, grabbed the tickets and walked down the aisle to a pair of seats.

"We need to change in town." He said.

"Fine." She sat down and closed her eyes. "Let me know when we're getting off."

By all their bones she was tired and the pain was beginning to overwhelm her. The dull throb of her bruises counterpointing with the sharp jabbing from her finger. Her techniques were for battlefield trauma, distractions and tricks to divert her mind from the reality until she got medical aid, she wasn't sure how much longer she could have endured the torture, another couple of fingers and they would have broken her. The boy had saved her.

A boy!

Now it had come to this, escaping on a bus, Marshall would piss himself if he caught them.

John sat beside her feeling, what? Not much. He thought he would be exhilarated at rescuing her, but instead he just felt tired, and scared, and worried that his parents would find out. He glanced over at Cam, was she worth it? The sweatshirt had ridden up her thigh exposing smooth light brown skin. Perfect he thought, the most beautiful woman he had ever seen. Not that he had seen many in real life but still. She was amazing and she had said they could fuck. But she was getting on a train and he would never see her again. Perhaps she would come back to see him?

"Ha." He laughed out loud.

She opened her eyes. "Something funny?"

"Not really."

"Hmm." Eyes shut again, head rocking to the movement of the bus. Her hair was loose and framed her face, making it seem younger and softer than when they first met. When she was beating the shit out of that guy. Blood stained the bandage on her hand making him think again of that room, of what had been done to her. He felt bile rise up, clenched his hand over his mouth and hoped he wouldn't spew. He focused instead on the route display and counted the stops.

"We're here." John said, thumbed the 'STOP' button on the bar in front of them.

Cam's eyes snapped open, looking around, confusion fading when she realised where she was and that she was free.

For the moment.

They got off on the same street he had asked the whores for directions, he doubted any would remember him but he hurried her to one of the pawn brokers and stopped outside it.

"Here." He took the money out of his pocket and handed it to her.

"What's this for?"

"Buy some clothes, shoes."

"I would rather use it on a train ticket."

"I've got a card for that."
"Yeah?"
"Yeah."
She looked at the sign. "They sell clothes here?"
"They take anything you want to pawn, they sell it when you don't buy it back."
She shook her head. "Gambling is for fools. Better to make your own money."
"Or steal it?"
She grinned. "Good, more of those balls, I like that in a man."
She reached out and cupped his nuts, stroked her hand up his stiffening cock.
"And I particularly like that."
He blushed red, stood there with nothing to say.
She laughed and walked into the store, he followed her after a minute, found her rifling through the racks, checking size and price, grabbed a skirt, raised an eyebrow at the shoes.
"Someone would pawn flip-flops?"
"If it gets them enough to play the slots."
She picked them up.
"These will do, I'm not giving any more money to these leeches than I have to."
She took them and the skirt to the security grille, handed over some cash and waited for her change. She dropped the shoes on the floor and pushed her feet in, still carrying the skirt as they left, ducked into an alley and pulled it on with a displeased look.
"Not sure I want someone's dirty clothes this close to my cunt but by their bones I wasn't going to buy second hand pants."
"I'm sure they wash them."
"Hmm."
Embarrassed by her saying cunt, making him think of hers, making walking difficult again.

"The bus stop is over there."

Another journey, she had the money now so he had to ask her to pay, the driver commenting on him being up late on a school night.

"Fuck to do with you?"

Cam said taking the tickets and walking down the aisle. They sat near the back this time.

"How long to the station?" She said.

"Ten minutes."

"And the next train?"

He looked at his Perse. "Oh, eight minutes."

She scowled. "And the one after?"

"Two hours."

"Fuck." Well it would have to do, at least she would be in a public place, though if what Marshall had said about owning the cops... would he even think of looking for her there? The slowest getaway in history. She laughed.

"Something funny?"

"Everything is fucking funny kid, it's just a matter of perspective."

Kid! It's bad enough that they weren't going to have sex - after she had promised him! But to keep calling him kid as well.

"John, my name is John."

She smiled. "I know your name." She put her hand on his thigh.

'Oh no here we go again' he thought.

"Look, John, I appreciate what you did for me. It took a lot of guts, I'll make it up to you. It won't be tonight, but if I ever get out of this fucking town I will come back when I can."

Like fuck she would, once she was out of here that was it. Sometimes you just had to leave it. It had cost her a finger to learn that lesson.

He looked into her eyes. "I'll never see you again."

Averted his face, trying not to cry.

Joe Mansour

She squeezed his leg, smiling at the bulge in his trousers.

"No John, I guess you won't."

He turned from her, concentrated on counting down the stops. Well that was it, she would be gone soon, she could have lied to him, given him some hope, he had risked his life for her!

She looked out of the window, watched the streets go past, determined never to see them again. Should she have lied to the kid? Was there any point? He had saved her life, something she felt deeply uncomfortable about, she owed him and didn't like to be in anyone's debt. As long as Marshall lived she wouldn't come back here. 'Face it, you're scared' she thought. Too fucking right she was, that had been the worst, worse than California, worse than Namibia, Thailand and New Zealand put together. Still, she could send him some money, the kid wanted to fuck her but a few grand would do instead, enable him to buy a car, impress a classmate, get him laid that way.

"Two more stops."

"Huh?"

"Two more to the train station, I've got my mums credit card, you can use it to buy a ticket." He gave her it, she spun the plastic round in her hand.

"The pin?"

"2207, my birthday."

"Ah, yeah, next month isn't it? I'll send you a present."

"Don't bother."

He glared at her, this was a mistake, he just wanted to go home.

The rest of the journey was in silence except for the hiss of air brakes and the muttering of other passengers. Approaching their stop John stood, walking down the moving bus not waiting for her to follow him. They got off in front of the train station. He glanced at his Perse.

"The ticket office will be shut, but there's machines in the foyer."

"Get back on the bus John."

"No. I'll see you in, make sure the card works. Besides that's not my bus - I've got five minutes till mine."

"OK, suit yourself."

She went in to the station and over to the ticket machine, knocked on the screen to wake it up.

"London, single."

"Two hundred and fifty nine pounds please." It said in a gender neutral voice.

"Shit." John muttered.

Cam displayed the card and tapped the pin in when requested.

"The train leaves in 1 hour and 56 minutes, thank you for your custom."

It intoned, a ticket dropping into the tray below the screen. She pocketed it.

"Two hours then - they got a bar?"

John pointed. "Over there."

She handed him the card back. "Well this is it."

"Yes."

She leant forward and kissed him, causing the world to spin away, he was oblivious to her wincing from his lips pressing against her bruised ones, he pushed his tongue into her mouth, surprised when hers probed back. He reached round and felt her arse, running his hands over it and pulling her hard against his body.

She broke off, stepping back from him.

"Thank you John, it's best if you go home. I doubt Marshall will come back to your house but if he does you know nothing right? He is a killer, he will have no compunction over killing you and your family. Do you understand me?"

"Sure."

Hell of a way to get rid of an erection, he would have no problem walking away now.

"Good bye Cam."

"Good bye John."

Leaving the station he glanced over his shoulder, disappointed when he saw she had gone, headed off to the bar.

He waited at the stop, just wanting to be home.

Four

Two hours later he woke, eyes closed, listening. The room quiet, the expected sound of another person breathing at his side absent.

Alone, he opened them and pushed up onto his elbows, looking round.

"Maya?"

He rolled off the bed dropping to a crouch and drawing his gun in one smooth movement. He straightened up and crossed to the door, checked the screamer was still armed. That left the bathroom, the door was shut, blocked by something leaning on the other side, he pushed harder, moving it in by a couple of centimetres.

"Hang on." Maya said.

Her voice groggy, she shifted out of the way and stood up allowing the door to open.

"What were you doing?" He holstered the pistol, eyes narrowed, suspicious.

"Sleeping." She rubbed her face, turned to the mirror and checked her reflection, wiped some of the drool from around her mouth.

"On the bathroom floor?"

She shrugged. "You were on the bed."

He shook his head. "Get up, we have some work to do."

"Work?" Alarm in her eyes, wondering what he was going to ask her to do next.

"Yeah, we're going to go back to that place where Lennon took his collections."

"Oh OK." She nodded. "And then?"

"I'm going to kill them."

Not sure if he was joking she said.

"Kill them?"

He lit a cigarette, offered her the pack. She took one, bent her head to let him light it.

"Yeah, well probably, we'll see how it goes. Get ready, we leave in five minutes."

"OK." She dropped her jeans to her knees and sat on the toilet. He left the room before she started to piss. 'Shy this one', she thought, finishing up and coming out. He went in, pushing the door closed behind him.

'Yeah, shy.'

Gareth Rockwell pulled into the car park outside the hotel and switched off the engine. He sat rolling the wedding ring around his finger thinking about what he was about to do, the betrayal he was about to commit, that he had been doing almost weekly for the past year. It wasn't that he didn't love his wife, that he wasn't happy in his life with her, but it just didn't have that spark any more. Besides, he didn't want to bother her, having two kids under 5 was hard, she didn't need him mithering her as well. He was smart enough to see through the excuses but that wouldn't stop him going into the hotel, booking a room and asking at reception for some extra pillows to be sent up. That was part of the thrill, not picking the woman himself, a lucky dip, a dip anyway.

Getting out the car he looked round, there was a slim chance that he would meet anyone he knew this side of town, but he had no justification for being here, the excitement of being found out, that was part of it. He had finished work early, his wife wouldn't expect him home for another hour, long enough, long enough to betray her and wash off the evidence. He buttoned his jacket and walked to the entrance, noticing a couple coming out heading towards him. A dead faced young man and a woman, more a girl, baggy sweatshirt, jeans leg's rolled up. What was a couple doing here at an hour-stop? Maybe they wanted some time together, both lived with the parents, needed somewhere to have sex? The man stopped in front of Gareth blocking his way, oh no, he'd been caught looking, he didn't need confrontation, perhaps he should just turn back now, leave it for today?

"You like what you see?" The man said, chin pushed out, questioning.

"What? I don't, I mean I."

Gareth tried to walk past, stopped when the man grabbed him by the arm.

"The girl, you like what you see?"

"I, no, I wasn't looking."

"It's OK, I know why you're here, fifty to fuck her."

The girl turned to the man, mouth open, about to say something. He held up his hand to her.

"I'm sorry, what?" Gareth said.

"That's what you're here for isn't it? You want a whore - well you can have her for fifty."

"You a pimp?"

"You interested?"

"That's very reasonable."

"There's a catch, I get to watch."

"Oh."

That was weird, but fifty was a great price, and the girl was pretty. Younger than he was used to, with a sullen look on her face, she had a rabbit rucksack on her shoulder, she was too young, wasn't she? But fifty, half the usual. Could he do it with another man there?

Maya glared at Chris, was this the better life he had

promised her? She should have known he was like the rest, just using her to make some money. Well he could fuck the John himself, see how he liked the taste of an old man's cock.

"Well?" The man said.

Gareth rolled the ring around his finger.

"OK, yes."

"Good. Go hire a room for a couple of hours, we'll be waiting."

Gareth walked off to the reception, still not sure that this was a good idea, but excited anyway, maybe this was the thrill he had been missing, could he get it up with another man watching? Would he want to join in?

"What the fuck do you think you are doing?" Maya said to Chris.

"We need a car, his will do."

"And I have to fuck him to get it?"

"I told you, there's another way."

"What?" She paled. "Kill him?"

"We'll see how it goes."

Fear washed over, drowning out the remaining Grind effects. He hadn't even flinched when he killed Lennon, a stranger to him, like this man here, an inconvenience, nothing more.

Gareth returned, a key grasped in his hand, nervous, not sure if this is what he wanted. If this was going too far, but if it had just been about sex then he could get that at home, this was about more, about the danger and excitement, the thrill of the forbidden.

"I've got it - room 101." He said.

"Let's go then." The man said, heading back to the motel.

Gareth looked at Maya, she sighed and muttered.

"Come on then."

Walked away without waiting for Gareth who stood, key in hand, watching them. He made his decision and rushed to catch up, joining them outside the room.

"Give me the key."

The man said, taking it from Gareth and opening the door. He gestured for Maya and Gareth to go in then followed, pulling the door shut after them. He dropped his bag and stepped behind Gareth, his arm coming round the man's throat in a choke hold cutting off his air. Gareth panicked, fighting for breath, flailing his limbs, trying to kick out, break free from the grip. Maya watched them, eyes wide, hand pressed to her mouth. The man held him tighter, waited for the struggling to cease, dropped the body to the floor.

"Is he dead?" Maya said.

"Shouldn't be, be out for a few minutes, that's all."

He squatted and removed Gareth's shoes, pulled off his socks and stuffed one in to the man's mouth. He used more of the rope from the bag to tie his hands and feet.

"Will he be OK?" Maya said, hovering near the pair of them, nervous energy making her shift from foot to foot.

"He might choke on his vomit."

"He might die?"

"Yes."

He searched through the man's pockets, pulled out the car keys, thought about taking the wallet, decided against it, he had enough money, no point in further ruining the guy's day.

"He'll be parked out front."

He left without looking back. Maya stared down at Gareth, trying to think, to process all of this. Chris had just mugged a man, a civilian, someone the police would care about not a lowlife scumbag like Lennon. She should run, just go.

But again the question was to where?

Maya gave an apologetic shrug to the unconscious man, left the room closing the door behind her. She caught up with Chris in the car-park where he was waving the fob around waiting for the chirrup. He spotted the vehicle and called her over, opened the driver's door, slinging his bag between the seats into the back. Maya got in the passenger's side. He punched the ignition and pulled out of the car-park, jerking through the junction heading back the way they had come. He lit a cigarette and chucked the pack to her.

"Tell me about Marshall's place." He said.

"And that was it? Man on the door, one in the foyer, four in the office?" He said, pulling up a couple of blocks down from the building.

"Yes."

"OK."

He reached back into the bag and pulled out the rope. Afraid of what he might do, that he was going to tie her up, she shied away, pressing against the door, one hand scrabbling for the handle. He ignored her, cut a length and tied the machine pistols to each end, looping it around his neck. The muzzles hanging out from the hem of his jacket wouldn't be that noticeable.

"Am I coming in with you?"

She didn't want to, she wanted to get away. Would he be taking the bag in with him? There was a lot of money in there, if he left it she could grab it and run.

"No, it's best if you wait in the car, I won't be long."

He got out and walked away without looking back. She sat, uncertain what to do, glancing back at the bag, all that money, it would be enough to get away, to the next county at least, or even London. There she could start again, or more likely fall back into prostitution, the money spent and her old life resumed.

He hoped she would be gone, he had left the money there to tempt her, to solve the problem and remove his obligation. Whatever, it wasn't something to dwell on now, he had a task to do. He pushed the buds into his ears and started his Perse playing, speeding up he walked towards the man guarding the entrance, thickset, wearing a bulky coat that suggested a hidden weapon. He reached in to the inner pocket of his jacket pulling out a taser, pressing the prongs against the man's neck and triggering it. The guard shuddered from the jolt, collapsed to the ground. He used it again on the electronic lock, shorting it out, pushed the door open and entered the building, brought up the left hand machine pistol and shot Bairamov in the face. He crossed to the inner door, kicked it open and tossed in a flashbang, counted to 3 and dived in to the room, coming up out of his roll with a pistol in each hand, checking target locations, firing at the first, Yates, dazed from the grenade, machine gun hanging limp from its shoulder strap. He slid over the desk and emptied the left clip in to Maeda. Letting it drop free he brought up the other tracking Wheeler trying to crawl from the room, pulled the trigger dropping him.

Hake roared, slam fired the shotgun, friend and foe both at risk from the swinging barrel blasting in to the room. He rolled, trying to get a better angle, his shoulder aching from a buckshot strike, dropped behind one of the desks, shredded bills raining down on him. He reloaded and fired under the table, taking out Hake's legs, stood up to check all threats were neutralised.

He turned down the music and walked over to where Wheeler lay wheezing on the floor, hands pressed to his stomach trying to stop his guts falling out.

"Help me." Wheeler said.

"Painful, good chance of infection." He said, reloaded his pistols and let them drop to his sides.

"Want me to take the pain away?"

"Please, don't, who? Please."

He squatted. "OK, you can pass on a message."

"What? Who?" Eyes glazed with pain, beginning to lose consciousness.

"Hey!" He slapped Wheeler's face. "Less of that, pay attention!"

"What? I, I, what?"

"Tell Marshall that this is a message from Cam."

"Cam?"

"Yes."

"You're Cam?"

"No, this is a message from Cam."

"Cam." Wheeler said and passed out.

"Shit."

Ah well, it didn't really matter. He stood, picked up a couple of the money packs off the nearest table, tucked them under his arm. If Maya had gone he would need the cash.

And if she hadn't?

He shrugged, no point worrying about it. He flicked tracks to something more calming, lit a cigarette. Outside he stepped over the writhing guard and headed back to the car.

That it was where he had left it had been expected, he had been sure she would've just taken the money. He opened the door and looked in, a sour smile when he saw her sat in the passenger seat, still his problem. He got in and tossed the money at her.

"Here you go – present for you."

He started the car and pulled out onto the road.

She held the bundles on her lap, tried to work out how much was in them, did he mean it? Was it for her? She could do anything with that much money, how much Grind she could buy!

"Did you kill someone?" She said.

"A couple, couple more will live."

"Why did you do it?"

"To send a message."

"To Marshall?"

"Yes."

"What was the message?"
"That I am coming for him."
"That's it?"
"Yes."
"And now what?"
"We check into a hotel and I get some rest, then we go and kill Marshall."

She ran her finger along the side of a pack, he didn't have a plan, that much was obvious from how they had got the car, he just made it up as he went along. She watched him drive, relaxed, paying little attention to the road, letting the automatics do most of the work, that seemed to be his nature, to just go with the flow. This wasn't any better than working the street, at least you knew what your day was going to bring, being treated like a piece of meat, but at least you knew. The fear was in the background, hidden by the drugs, there were three shots left, she should have taken the money and run, why was she still with him?

"You said you would take me with you." She said.
"Hmm?"

He lit a cigarette, passing her the pack. She took one and paused to light it before continuing.

"You said you would take me with you, when you left, after."
"Yes."
"Where would we go?"
"I don't know, where do you fancy?"
"And then what?"
"Hmm?" He glanced at her, knocked some ash out of the window.
"What would we do?"
"We?"
"You said."
"I said I would take you out of here, after that it's up to you."
"But what would I do?"

He waved his hand, a dismissive gesture. "Whatever you wanted."

"That's it?"

"What do you want me to say?"

"I don't know, that you have a plan, that you're not just aimlessly drifting through life."

He laughed. "And what the fuck are you doing?"

"Well." She squirmed in her seat. "I never said I had one."

"Neither did I."

"No, but."

"Look, what do you want?"

"Something more than this."

He pulled over to the side of the road, turned to her and said.

"I can't offer you anything more than this, when I have dealt with Marshall we will leave. Then it's up to you."

"Up to me?"

"Yes, I'll give you some money, you can be on your way, or."

"Or?"

He threw the stub out of the window, rubbed his face. What was he doing? What was he thinking? He was lonely, he missed Cam. But this woman wasn't a replacement for her, she couldn't be, she shouldn't be. He sighed and took the packet from her, lit a cigarette.

"Or?" She asked again.

"Or, I'll train you, show you how to make your money in a different way, travel to new places and kill people."

He smiled, stared into her eyes, noticed the fear and the revulsion, wondered what he was doing. Imagined Cam shaking her head at his idiocy. He didn't give her chance to reply, instead he opened the driver's door and got out, used the handle of his pistol to smash in the rear quarter window. She flinched at the noise, mouth open in surprise. He got in and started the car, pulled back out in to traffic.

"What the fuck?" She said, brushing slivers of glass from her clothes.

"You'll see."

He pulled into a petrol station stopping by the pump furthest from the kiosk, grabbed the bag out the rear and dumped it in her lap. Unzipping it he took out a wad of notes from his bank heist, broke the band on them and stuffed them in his pocket.

"Back in a minute." He said, getting out.

He fed some of the money into the pump and jabbed the nozzle through the rear window, pulled the trigger spraying petrol, soaking the back seat, liquid pooling and dripping down in to the footwell, the fumes choking Maya.

"What the hell are you doing?"

She coughed, hands clasped to her mouth.

He ignored her, keeping the flow going until the credit had run out, put the nozzle back and got in the driver's seat.

"Open your window." He said.

"Are you crazy! What the fuck are you doing?"

"You'll see, won't be long, just don't have a cigarette."

He laughed, she glared at him, what was he playing at? The car stunk and it made breathing difficult, her eyes red and stinging, his the same. He ignored the discomfort, driving another couple of kilometres in to town, stopping near a parade of shops.

"OK, shove all that money in the bag and get out."

"Why?"

"Just wait for me here."

Glad to be out she stood on the kerb, the bag at her feet and watched him pull away, accelerating towards the betting shop on the corner.

Mounting the kerb he blared his horn, ploughing into the bookies front window, the airbag inflating in his face, side bags pinning him until he slashed them with his knife, he stumbled out, pulled the remaining money from his pocket. He lit it and tossed the burning notes into the car. Feeling the heat build at his back he left by the main door.

Open mouthed Maya stared at the scene before her, the car embedded in the front of the shop, smoke beginning to billow around it. People struggling to get out, Chris walking over to her seemingly oblivious to the chaos around him. He bent to pick up the bag and slung it over his shoulder. He smiled.

"Not the best place to hang around."

Minus Seven

"Puretones and a lager – that one."

Pointing at the pump. She had never heard of it but, as long as it wasn't what they called beer over here, it would do. The bar was empty, just her and the man serving, he poured her a pint and placed the cigarettes next to it. She handed over a couple of the notes, split the seal on the pack and took one out.

"You got a light?"

The barman handed over a disposable and took back some of her change. She lit her cigarette, picked the glass up and went to a booth. She sat facing the door, keeping an eye on the screen showing departures. Two fucking hours, this was getting ridiculous. Her body ached, interspersed with sharp spikes of pain from her hand. Two hours, did Marshall know she had escaped? Had he come back to continue with her torture? What would he do? What would she do in his position? Well, she would figure that the escapee would get out of town as fast as possible, steal a car maybe, but to sit in a station bar waiting for a train? She shook her head, smoke curling from her lips, a sip of beer, fighting the urge to sleep. It was doubtful he would go to John's house, the boy and his family were safe, he wouldn't be on her conscience. She looked in distaste at her hand, blood oozing through the bandage, the stump a bitter reminder of what Marshall would do, liked to do.

No, the boy would be fine.

She drew hard on the cigarette and tried to ignore the nagging doubt, eyes flitting between the screen and the door, waiting, nothing else she could do.

He paid with the last of his money. The bus would take him to the end of his street and with luck he would be able to sneak back in unnoticed. Until his mum got her next credit card bill, nearly three hundred pounds! What was he going to say? Maybe he should blame Cam, say she must have stolen it, maybe he shouldn't put it back, maybe he should have left her it. But he had been angry and annoyed and wanted to punish her in some way. For being so ungrateful, he had saved her life! And soon she would be gone and it would be back to the same old humdrum existence, his brief moment of excitement over, returning to the usual dead end days, revising for exams, squabbles with his parents, trying to get a feel of Bryony's boobs and sneaky wanks in the bathroom.

Sirens howled, the bus slowed pulling to the side of the road to allow a police car to pass, remained stationary for an ambulance followed by another two cop cars, causing chatter amongst the bus passengers speculating on what had happened, prompting searches on Perses for local news. John resisted looking at his, he'd had enough excitement for the night. He got up, waved at the driver to open the door. Getting off he pushed buds in to his ears, picked a playlist, jammed his hands in to his coat pockets and cut through the estate heading to his house.

Passing the place he had watched Cam fighting (had that only been a few hours before?) he became aware of the emergency vehicles, their lights pulsing, reflected in the windows. It was on his street, an accident or something, he quickened his pace, stopping when he saw they were parked outside his home. Dread welling up he began to panic, it was his house, if it had just been the police then it would have been

OK, most likely explanation his parents had called them when they found he was missing. But an ambulance, someone was hurt, or worse. Had Marshall come looking for Cam?

Were his parents OK?

Neighbours were out standing around in groups, attracted and excited by the noise. The woman from the house opposite was stood on the pavement taking in the scene, arms crossed over her velvet dressing gown, matching slippers poking out of the hem. Reluctant to approach the house he walked over to her instead.

"Mrs Grenady, what's happened?"

"Johnny! Is that you?"

She reached out to grab him, bony, thin hands gripping his arms near the shoulder, face leaning in to his.

"It's your parents Johnny. They..."

She released him, stepped back, face showing mixed emotions, hard for the boy to read.

"Johnny, we heard gunshots, it was like on a Thread, Mr Donals went over to check, Johnny, he said, no perhaps it's best for you to speak to the police."

"Mrs Grenady, what is it?"

"The police will tell you."

Two stretchers were brought out of his house, he ignored the woman, pushed her questing hand away, straining to look but unwilling to get closer, fearful of what he would see.

"Mrs Grenady, my parents, are they all right?"

"I'll take you over to the police."

His knees buckled, the ground seeming to soften under him.

"They're dead aren't they?"

He staggered backwards, leant against a hedge.

"Both of them dead?"

She nodded, put her hand on his shoulder.

"I'm sorry Johnny. Where have you been? The police will want to talk to you."

"Dead."

He bent over and threw up, spewing vomit into the bushes. Could it be true, could they be dead? He straightened and wiped phlegm from his mouth, looked towards his house, the windows lighting up from the camera flashing in the front room. He should go and speak to the police, this had to be Marshall's work, Cam - was she all right? Ashamed by that thought, his parents were dead, because of him, because of her. What should he do? Marshall said he owned this town, owned the cops, should he hand himself in? Would Marshall kill him too? Probably, or torture Cam's whereabouts from him. He glanced at his Perse, her train left in an hour, if he laid low till then it wouldn't matter, it would be too late for Marshall to find her. But his parents would still be dead, and what of him?

"Johnny?"

"I'm sorry Mrs Grenady." He turned and ran back down the street.

The beer was going to her head, not having eaten for a day, plus the beating and the blood loss had severely lowered her tolerance. She grinned and lit a cigarette from the embers of her last. Thirty five minutes to go, the display showing her train was on time. She thought the joke about this country was that the trains were always late.

Almost the fuck out of here.

Maybe get some fresh air, clear her head a little. She needed a piss but these Brits didn't like you to use their toilets, you had to get a code for the door. She eased out from the booth, winced when she caught her hand on the table edge, stood for a moment while she controlled the pain, not long now, not long.

The door swung open, the kid, John stood in the entrance.

"Cam." His face tear stained, voice broken. "Cam, they killed my parents."

Cigarette tumbling from her fingers, she crossed the floor to him. John stood, shaking, breathing in half choked sobs. The barman looked up from his Perse, watching them.

She hissed. "Be quiet."

Her mind racing, Marshall had gone to John's home, gone looking for the boy. Why? When he had found she was missing he must have gone to the house, found the boy gone, killed the parents. If he was as connected as he said then the train ticket was useless. She grabbed John by the elbow and marched him out of the bar.

"Cam?" He looked bewildered.

"Quiet till we get out of here."

He was crumbling, falling apart, she could see it in his face. They left the station, she led him in to an alley, stopped, turned and slapped him. Shocked, he reeled back, hand to his cheek.

"Cam!"

"What the fuck did you think coming here?"

He had saved her life, again, she would have sat in that bar, ignorant of the danger until Marshall strolled in to take her back to that room.

"I didn't think, I don't know, I came to tell you, to warn you. What shall we do?"

We? She should kill him, leave his body here for Marshall and the cops to find. Open and shut case, suicide, easy to do, broken glass and slashed wrists. They wouldn't look further.

She owed him though, he had saved her life, she owed him.

"We're even." She said, dragging him along. "Let's get out of here. Where do the whores hang out?"

"Um, I don't know." He blushed, remembering. "There were some on Jacqueline, near the casino."

"Another bus?"

She smiled, stopped in front of him, took his other hand and stared in to his eyes. "Focus John, and we will get out of this. I need you to be focused."

"Yes, a bus." He nodded in the direction of the shelter.

"Come on." She dropped his hands and turned from him, walked away. He stood watching her, helpless, not sure what to do.

"John."

"Coming."

"So this is the place?"

She looked up and down the street, noted the women on the corners, the cars driving slowly along it.

"Yes." He said, wondering what they were doing there.

She took his arm leading him in to an alley.

"OK." She said.

She pulled her sweatshirt up and knotted it under her breasts, rolled the waistband down on her skirt, pulling it up to make it shorter, just covering her arse.

"I look like a whore?"

He thought she looked incredible, desire bubbling up, making him uncomfortable, conflicting with the grief. What was she going to do? Earn money by prostituting herself? Be fucked by fat greasy men? Suck their cocks? How could she?

"Well?"

"Yeah, you look like a whore."

"Good, stay here till I come back for you."

She walked over to the kerb, trying to look provocative despite the dirty shirt and bandaged hand. Still, she didn't have many options, she needed to get out of town and this was the fastest way.

A car pulled up and the window wound down, she leant on the frame and gave what she thought was a sexy smile.

"You want some?" She said, winked at the leering man.

"How much?"

"Forty?"

"Get in."

He must have thought it was his birthday, she had no idea

what they charged but by his reaction it was a lot more than that. She opened the door, slid onto the seat, reached her hand between his legs and squeezed his balls.

"Let's go somewhere quiet, there's an alley up ahead." She said pointing to the one where John was waiting.

"OK." He said and followed her directions.

Horrified, John ducked behind a dumpster, was he going to have to listen to them doing it? The car pulled up in front of where he was hiding and stopped.

"This'll do." Cam said, gave the man another squeeze. "Turn off the engine."

He complied, unbuttoned his trousers and unzipped the fly.

"OK, suck it." He said.

She raised her arm pointing forward, puzzled he peered through the windscreen. She brought her elbow back fast striking him in the face. He squealed and rocked forward in pain, hands to his nose. She grabbed the back of his head and smashed it into the steering wheel causing the horn to blare on each strike. She pulled the man's head back, venting her frustration and rage on him, punching him in the face until the pain from her hand made her stop. She wiped her bloody fists on the front of his shirt and got out of the car. John ran out from his hiding spot, shock and confusion on his face, unable to process the events.

"Give me a hand." She said, walking round to the driver's side and opening the door. She yanked the unconscious man out of the seat, dragged him to the back of the car. Still trying to comprehend what he had seen John followed her .

"Let's get him in the trunk." She said, popping it open.

John bent to grab the legs and they manoeuvred him in.

"Is he dead?" He said.

"Not at the moment."

"What are you doing?"

"Stealing a car, what did you think I was going to do? Fuck

them for money?"

She sucked through her teeth.

"Get in, I'll be a minute."

She rooted through the man's pockets, took out his cash and tucked it in to her skirt pocket. If she dumped him in the alley he might be found before they got out of the county, best to take him with them, they might even need him if they ran out of fuel. She slammed the lid down, got in the driver's side and tapped the dashboard screen to wake it up, scrolled to the SatNav.

"London." She said, waited for the map to find their location. It resolved into an arrow, a melodious voice saying. "Make a U-turn when possible."

She started the engine and backed the car out of the alley, joined the light traffic heading out of town.

John sat in the passenger seat, distracted he pulled the belt across his shoulder snapping it home. This was all going too fast, he was just a kid, still in school, his biggest worry was if Becky Felzler thought he was cool. Now look at him, in a stolen car on the way to London, the owner unconscious in the boot. After breaking into a house and rescuing a woman, after going home to find his parents murdered. Murdered, it couldn't be true could it? Were they really dead? Maybe he should turn himself in, face the music, maybe he should ask Cam to stop and let him out. She would be gone then, and he, no one would believe him, he would go to prison, it couldn't be true.

John tapped the screen, ignoring Cam's scowl he switched it to news and scrolled down to local, found the story, double murder, bludgeoned to death, son the likely suspect, extremely dangerous, approach with caution, his school photo leering out; the wanted had no rights to privacy. He switched it back to the map.

"Shit."

"Trouble?"

Cam said, her eyes on the road.

"My, my parents, they say that I, that I."

He put his hands to his face.

"John?"

"It says they were bludgeoned, I don't understand."

"Understand what?"

"Mrs Grenady said she heard gunshots."

She nodded.

"That Marshall is a motherfucker."

"What?"

"Not likely you would have a gun in your house, straight up people like you, so the report is altered, means he has someone in the police, or the press or both."

She pulled out a cigarette, threw the pack at him.

"Have one, calm you down."

It calmed her but would probably fuck him up, keep his mind off his parents though. Distracted he fumbled the pack open, took one out and pushed in the lighter on the dash. When it popped she turned her head and he pressed the glowing coil against the tip, his eyes on her, she nodded, exhaled a cloud of smoke. He put his between his lips and lit it. Harsh choking cough and streaming eyes. He felt sick, now knew what they meant by green to the gills. People enjoyed this? The buzz made him feel light headed but there was nothing pleasant about it. He stubbed it out in the ashtray and cracked his window to let in some air.

She laughed.

"First time is always the worst, like anything worthwhile, you have to work at it."

The SatNav guided them through the town heading for the motorway, no signs of road blocks or increased patrols. Maybe Marshall had been bluffing about his influence, whatever, soon as she crossed the county line they could breathe a little easier, if the local cops were looking for a boy then it was doubtful they would think he had the wherewithal to steal a car. They would be checking the bus and train stations in case he tried to run, more likely they would believe he was hiding out at a friends house or huddled somewhere frightened and alone.

Ten minutes later they drove down the slip road on to the motorway, Cam engaged the cruise control and took her hands off the wheel letting the automatics take over. She tilted her chair back and lit a cigarette.

"You smoke a lot." John broke the silence, wanting the distraction from his thoughts.

"Yeah I do."

"Aren't you worried about getting cancer?"

"Why? It's curable."

"Yes, but still."

"Why deny yourself the pleasure for what might never be?"

"I guess."

"You guess?" She tsked.

"What does that mean?"

"You ask a lot of questions."

"If you don't ask questions how do you learn anything?"

"If you spend all your time asking questions when do you have the time to understand the answers?"

"What?"

"Shut up or I'll put you in the trunk with that guy."

"What are we going to do with him?"

"We'll dump the car in London, he'll be found sometime, or suffocate, whatever."

"Don't you care?"

"About him? No."

"About anyone?"

"Me."

"That's it, no one else?"

"What else is there?" She looked at him, smoke boiling from her nostrils. "It's the only thing that matters."

"Why am I here then?"

"I told you I owed you, this makes us even, if I'd left you then you'd have been arrested, handed over to Marshall, tortured whether you knew anything about me or not."

"I wouldn't have told him anything."

"Wouldn't you? Then you're a fool, I'd have told them anything they wanted to hear to save my skin."

"Then why didn't you?"

"Because I knew I was dead if I did."

"That doesn't make sense."

"Welcome to the real world John. None of it makes fucking sense."

It started to rain, eliciting a grunt from Cam which John, fed up with the half answers she gave, didn't query. They drove in silence, punctuated by the scrape of the windscreen wipers and the occasional update from the SatNav.

John switched the screen back to a news feed, the main story about a politician caught selling favours, the reporter feigned shock at such behaviour then cut to the House of Representatives where the accused was trying to defend her position before a blurred mass of hooting outrage.

"Why is she the only one not obscured?" Drawn in to the drama, Cam had been puzzled by the pixelated faces.

"Celebrity act of seventeen."

"What's that?"

"A law was passed that gave an individual the right to their image. It couldn't be reproduced or stored without permission. A side effect was that cameras became impractical as you needed the permission of every person you recorded."

"No cameras? What about in banks?"

"You'd have to sign a waiver before you went it, so most don't bother installing them, I think some places like the casinos use them but only to monitor, they're not allowed to record."

"Fucking mental, you banned cameras to protect famous people?"

"Well, all people, as all have the potential to become famous."

She nodded.

"You know a lot about it for something that happened before you were born."

"We did it in school, in history."

"Ah." School, she kept forgetting how young he was. A fucking kid, a fucking liability. She would set him up in London, a few thousand to get him started then she was done, he was on his own, dead or a junkie in six months, selling his mouth and arse for fixes. He wouldn't last a year if she left him in London, was that saving his life or just drawing out his death?

John watched the news, trying to control the panic, a couple of hours and they would be in London, then what? Would she just leave him there? At least he might now get to fuck her. He laughed out loud.

"Something funny?"

"This whole thing."

"Now you get it." She smiled, bruises lips and bloody teeth.

He flicked the screen back to the map, watched the miles count down for a while. Cam laid back in her seat with her eyes closed, lips mumbling nonsense around another cigarette.

"Are we staying in London?" He asked, hopeful that the answer would be we rather than him, a sign that she wasn't dumping him.

Irritated she opened her eyes "For as short as we can."

"And then?"

"We get out of the country."

We, his heart lifted, she glanced over and saw the hope on his face. She had decided to take him with her, at least to the Continent, set him up somewhere, boarding school or something. That would be the price of her life, they would be even then. Might even be better for him than growing up in Marshall's town, probably doing him a favour. Yeah, getting his parents killed, no doubt he would be grateful.

"John?"

"Yes?"

"Don't worry, you saved my life, I don't forget such things."

"OK."

What was she saying to him? None of this made sense, he had been carried along in the moment and now it was too late, wanted by the police, his parents dead.

His parents dead.

Tears streamed down his face.

His parents dead.

His breath shortened and broken with sobs.

What was this? Why was he crying?

"John?"

"I'm sorry." He gasped. "I can't help it."

"John?"

"My mum, my dad."

"Have a cigarette."

He scowled at her. Have a cigarette? Was that her answer to everything? It probably was, the way she smoked, one after the other, barely pausing between them, the car filling full of fumes, making him light headed, feeling sick. Oblivious, she sucked on the filter, eyes half closed, the smoke pluming out. She looked content, the past few hours forgotten, was that the way to live?

Cam was at a loss, she didn't know how to deal with his grief, her own was excised years ago, along with most other emotion. She guessed she should be sympathetic but she couldn't think of the words, wasn't even sure if she wanted to, would make it easier if the kid thought she was a heartless bitch. Well she was, wasn't she?

By their bones she was tired, the drone of the car should have sent her to sleep, but the combination of John's incessant questioning and the pain from her missing finger kept it tantalisingly out of reach. All she wanted was to be away from this country, put it behind her and move on. The boy was holding her back, tying her to memories she would rather forget. She lit a cigarette from the stub of the last and closed her eyes again.

False dawn from the floodlights on the great wall heralded their approach to London. Entry was limited to residents during curfew, all other cars filtered off to holding parks. Trying to glimpse the city John sat up and stared out the window, his imagination stoked by the images seen on Threads and Ent shows.

"Wow, it's amazing."

"Yeah, amazing what fear does to you."

Tired of her snide comments he decided not to ask her what she meant. Cam took control of the car and pulled off the motorway heading for a parking garage. She drove up to the top floor and pulled over into a space and switched off the engine.

"We'll have to wait until the city opens for business." She said, leant over to look in the glove box, rummaging through the crap she found a pair of sunglasses.

"These'll do."

"What about the man in the boot?"

"He'll be fine, it says max 12 hours stay, once it goes past that they'll check it out."

Or he'll die in there.

She got out, walked over to the lifts and pushed the call button, heard the slam of the other door and footsteps approaching. They rode it down, Cam leant against the wall checking the cash she had taken from the man, handy that he'd been looking for a whore, they had enough money to get some food and get into the city, or as far in as non-residents were allowed. Next to the car park was a rest-stop, inside the sole occupant was the man behind the bar, half asleep, she tapped to get his attention.

"Gin tonic and a pack of Puretones."

She looked at John and said.

"What do you want?"

"Uh? A Martini."

She laughed. "A Martini, what the fuck kind of drink is that?"

"James Bond drinks them."

"James Bond sounds like a pussy. And a Mr Fizzy."

"Mr Fizzy!" Did she think he was twelve? "I'll have a Snaffer."

"Snaffer then. When does the first bus go in?"

"In five minutes but that's utility workers and support staff, the eight thirty is the first that non-residents can use." The man said.

"Another fucking hour and a half." She shook her head. "Better give me another pack of Puretones then." She took them and headed to a booth, John following behind with the drinks.

He took a sip of his, grateful that the barman hadn't stuck a straw in it.

"What do we do when we get into London?" He said.

"We call Greves, he's got my money, he'll get us papers, get us on the train to France."

"I've already got I.D, got my card last birthday."

"You're going to need a new one, doubtful John McPhereson would be allowed to leave the country."

"A new one." A new identity, he wasn't sure about that, it was who he was, who his family was, and he was the last of them, he couldn't change his name, couldn't do that to them. He rotated the glass, chinking ice cubes together. She lit a cigarette, placed the packs on the table.

"And will you change yours?" He said.
"Yes."
"Is Cam your real name?"
"As much as it matters."
"I don't understand."
"Not this again."
"It's just that..."
"John, leave it."

He lapsed into silence, focused on his glass of Snaffer. She leant back and closed her eyes, strung out now, with the end so near, this is where it all went wrong. If Marshall suspected she would head for London, if he knew she had people there. He'd what? The police forces kept themselves separate, no crossing judicial lines. They might be after John but there was nothing on her. She was taking a risk with him, curse this fucking obligation, she should walk away, not look back.

"Cam?"

"Yes?" Irritated, what was it now?

"It's quarter past eight Cam, we should get the bus."

By their bones, she'd fallen asleep, no use worrying about it though.

"Be back in a minute."

She followed the sign to the toilets. Squinting in the bright wash-room lights she stood in front of the mirror assessing the damage. Eyes beginning to blacken, nose pointing off to one side, bruises forming on her face and arms. Well she could sort the nose, she pressed her hands against it and twisted it back, grunting at the crunch. Ran her head under the tap wetting her hair and sleeking it back. Unrolled the skirt, pulling it down to mid thigh and unknotted the sweatshirt. She put on the sunglasses and stared at her reflection.

"You look like a junkie whore." She muttered, but all she had to do was get on the bus.

She went back out to John, said. "You need it?"

He shook his head

"Another bus then." She said, lighting a cigarette.

Getting on the coach was straightforward, the driver, still groggy from the early morning start, had barely glanced at them, besides you only went into the city if you had the means, the vagrants were soon swept up and shipped off to holding camps. It was their problem, they didn't pay him enough to care.

Cam took the window seat and leant her head against it, keeping her eyes open, watching the road go by. Almost, almost, she didn't even want to hope, this was insufferable, every time she thought she was out and safe there was something more. The bus slowed for the gates, she imagined she could feel her teeth vibrating from the scanner sweeping over them, and people were worried about cigarettes when they happily sat in a giant x-ray machine so some minager could get their rocks off staring at naked bodies.

"This fucking country." She said.

"Sorry?"

"Nothing." It wasn't any worse than her own, or many of the others she had burnt her way through.

John peered past her, gawking at the city on the other side of the wall, the first buildings coming in to view after the cleared area. They were in the tourist zone, the residents hidden behind an inner wall that kept them safe from the terrors of the world. They passed gaudy signs and billboards advertising shows and events, a collection of gaggling and screeching hoardings, their images flashing and strobing to tempt and allure – 'British Science Museum presents Bang, Pops and Fizzes', 'Cats the Musical', 'Royal Academy: David Shrigley Retrospective', 'Lord Radcliffe, My Struggle, My Triumph' and others all vying for attention to take money from the excited day trippers on their visit to the old capital.

The bus dropped them off at the Covent Garden stop and

they joined the throngs of early morning tourists milling about waiting for the organised tours to start. Cam lit a cigarette and looked for a phone booth, spotting one she waved at John to follow her. She typed in a number and waited for the callee to accept the charges. The screen scrolled adverts and then faded to black, a single word 'connected' floating in the centre.

"Greves?" She said.

"Cam, I expected to hear from you a lot sooner, Christ you look a mess."

"Yes, not as clean cut as I hoped."

Laughter, the screen still blank. "You want your money?"

"Would be nice."

"I'll have to come and pick you up."

"I'll be waiting at the café." She read the name of the one closest to them. "'Threpenny Bit', hurry up I'm down to my last few dollars."

"Pounds, darling, pounds."

"Whatever, make it quick."

She closed the connection and turned to John. "Greves will meet us at the café."

"Who's Greves?"

"An associate, a cleaner, he takes your money and makes it clean."

"A money launderer?" He had seen them in Threads. "You get back twenty pee in the pound."

"It better be a fuck lot more than that."

"You swear a lot."

"I swear enough."

"What does that mean?"

She shrugged. "What does anything mean? Language isn't my strong point, smoking, killing, fucking, they're what I do."

"Really?"

She smiled.

"At least I didn't say fucking then killing."

Laughing she walked over to the Threpenny Bit café. Inside the décor was a designers idea of Dickensian London. A waiter dressed as a chimney sweep approached them.

"Two coffees, strong as you can. We'll be there." She said pointing to a table in the corner.

It would cost her but she could trust Greves, once he took them into the private zone she could relax, finally get some sleep.

The waiter brought them their drinks and she paid with the last of her cash. John tipped two cartons of milk and four sachets in to his. She shook her head and sipped her own, by their bones it was almost decent.

"Once we do get to Greves's we can take stock, get some breathing room, save your questions until then."

"OK." He tasted his coffee, grimaced and added another sugar.

"Cam, you look worse in the flesh than on the screen." A man stopped by their table, removed a pair of sunglasses and hung them from the breast pocket of a tailored suit. He smiled, crinkling the skin around brown eyes, the sentiment not reflected in them.

"Good to see you as well Greves." She stubbed out her cigarette and stood, motioning to John.

"This is John, an associate of mine."

"Rather young isn't he?"

John glared at the man, resenting his cool demeanour.

"He's old enough." She said.

"Is he? And is he coming with us?"

"Yes."

"Pricey."

"We'll talk about that later, I assume you have a car?"

"This way, if you're done?"

He led them outside, his car parked on double yellows with

its hazard lights flashing. He gestured to the back and she said to John. "Get in." Taking the front passenger seat for herself, Greves got behind the wheel, started the engine and pulled out into traffic.

"Can I smoke?" Cam said.

"I would rather you didn't."

She scowled and John watching Greves's face in the rear-view mirror caught the smile that flickered for a moment. It seemed to him that stopping Cam smoking was more to do with power than health.

Cam tapped the cigarette against the pack.

"So how much have I left?"

"From the ten million? Seven point eight."

"Fuck, what's that in something I can spend?"

"About six million Euros."

She nodded. "It will have to do, I need some ID cards, for me and the kid."

Kid, she'd said it again, John sat back in his seat and turned his head to look out of the window.

"Looks like someone has a crush on you." Greves commented, his smile getting broader.

She could have done with a cigarette, the pain was building again and she needed the distraction. "Proper one down to the bone."

"Expensive."

"I have some money."

"Well at the moment I have the money."

"Don't fuck with me Greves, I'll rip your fucking throat out."

He held his hands up. "Just joking Cam, just a joke."

"You need to work on your material."

She lit a cigarette, fuck him if he objected.

"Just get us to your place Greves, I need a shower and some sleep. We can talk after."

"Won't be long."

He frowned at the smoke and adjusted the air con.

London seemed little different from his home town and John soon tired of the scenery. They approached the inner wall, separated from the rest of the city by a cleared zone, the demolished buildings replaced by concrete blocks and cutter wire, the access controlled with choke points and automatic weapons. Greves slowed for the initial gate, keeping the speed low so that by the time he reached the second the first had closed, allowing that one to open. The other side looked little different to John, grimy buildings and narrow streets, maybe a few less bill boards but nothing really to show that this was where the residents of the second richest city in Europe lived.

"Here we go." Greves said.

They turned onto an apartment block access ramp, the gate swinging open at their approach.

"I have the top two floors here." Greves said, pulling in to a parking bay next to the lifts. He switched off the engine and got out. He pressed the call button, the doors opening immediately and he waved them into it. He pressed his thumb against the activation plate. A quiet hum, a slight sensation of movement, and the doors opened revealing a foyer, decorated in marble and gold, twin staircases curling round to the upper floor, a huge chandelier dominating the scene.

"Not bad." Cam said, thinking 'if you liked living in a gaudy whorehouse'.

"You got a place I can get cleaned up, crash for a few hours?" She said.

"Upstairs, on the left, Martha will show you - MARTHA!"

The last shouted at a woman coming in from a side door. "Ah Martha, please show my guests to a room. Or will you require two?"

John stared at her, wondering what she would say, hoping she would say no.

"One will do Greves." Ignoring the wry smile and the huge

grin.

"Get yourself refreshed then, I will see you in a few hours for lunch, say one pm?"

"Thank you." She turned to the waiting servant. "Where's this room then?"

In the shower, Cam let the water wash over her, the heat soothing away the pain, cursing when she caught the stump on her hand. She was safe now, Greves had no idea where she had been or where the money was from, she had made sure of that. He had no interest in selling her out, no one to sell her out to. He might press the kid, try and get something out of him, the main reason she wanted to keep him close. Ah, the kid, what about him? She had promised they would fuck, he seemed pretty keen on the idea. Still, what harm could it do? She stepped out of the shower reaching for one of the fluffy towels, drying off and putting on a robe. She wrapped the towel round her hair and flipped it back into a makeshift turban. On the sink were a couple of toothbrushes sealed in plastic, 'the consummate host', she thought, though she knew there would be a price tagged to her bill. She used one, glad to get the taste of old blood and cigarettes from her mouth, at least for a short while. Went back into the bedroom where John was sat on the edge of the bed. He looked up at her, desire filling him, the towel was a bit off putting as it was something his mum would do, but she would take it off, wouldn't she? This was it, he was going to have sex, he could feel his cock straining at his trousers, not sure whether he should try and hide it, or should he show his desire?

"Go take a shower John."

'This is it!' he thought 'This is it' pushing the bathroom door shut behind him, a smile beaming across his face. He undressed and got in the shower. Soaped up, better give his cock a good clean, perhaps he should masturbate, take the pressure off? But then what if he couldn't get it up again? He rinsed and stepped out the cubicle, using a towel to haphazardly dry his body, finished with a quick ruffle of his hair. But now what? Should he put his clothes back on? Or go out just in the robe like she had? That was probably better, he wrapped it round his waist, pinning his erection to his body and walked out the room. Cam was already in the bed, he sidled up to it and, dropping the gown to the floor, climbed under the duvet. Naked, he lay there, his cock throbbing, not sure what to do. Tentatively he reached out a hand and touched her side.

"Let me get some sleep John, we'll fuck when I wake up."

Damn, he pulled his hand away, he should have had that wank after all.

She woke, eyes closed, working out where she was, ah yes Greves's, comfortable bed, someone next to her, the boy, John; hard cock pressed against her thigh. She ran her fingers along it, well she had promised him and sex might be good to release some tension. He stirred at her grip, she opened her eyes to stare into his, he leant forward and kissed her. 'This is it', he thought, he was finally going to do it. He pushed his hand between her legs and started rubbing

"Not so hard." She said, breaking the kiss, and taking his hand, showing him how to do it, her hand moving in time with his. She rolled onto her back, pulling him on top, her hand guiding his cock into her.

'This is it, this is it' he thrust forward, juddered and came.

"Oh shit, I'm sorry, I."

She smiled, pushed him off her on to his side, reached for the cigarettes on the bedside table.

"Give it a few minutes and we'll try it again."

Greves was waiting for them in the dining room, the table

set for three, his plate already used with the cutlery laid across it. A coffee cup in one hand, he scanned the news on the pad in front of him. If he was annoyed by their lateness he kept it to himself.

"Good afternoon, rested I trust?" He said, gesturing to the chairs.

"Or didn't you sleep?" Smiling when John's face turned crimson.

"Martha will bring you food, just tell her what you want."

"I'll have what he had." Cam said, pointing at Greves's plate.

John said. "Yeah, the same for me."

Hoping it was something he would like.

Greves's smiled, nodded to the maid.

"Not too cramped in that bed?" He said.

John's face flushed, Cam lit a cigarette.

"It was fine Greves, you got what I asked for?"

"It's only been a few hours." He said, frowning at her smoking.

"Enough time for a man with your resources."

"True." He was vain enough to enjoy the compliment.

"They'll be ready tonight, I'll need to take the boy for a scan etc." He looked at John. "Don't worry it won't take as much fluid from you as Cam did."

John's face turned a darker shade, Cam shook her head, tapped ash on to a side plate.

Martha brought them soup, placing a bowl in front of each of them. John looked at it suspiciously, unsure about the colour, a pale brown unlike the red of his usual tomato. Cam set to it, her first real food in days, slurping soup in her haste, tearing chunks of bread and dipping them in.

"You should save room for the main course, it's lamb, it seems you have a thing for young meat." Greves said.

She grunted in reply, ran her finger round the bowl's edge, absent-mindedly licking it, John staring rapt, remembering that tongue and getting hard again. He felt Greves's eyes on him and turned to look, anger flashing at the sardonic grin.

"Ignore him John." She needed the money launderer, she was still at risk until she made it to the continent.

He took a mouthful of his soup which made him realise how hungry he was, began eating it at the same speed as Cam.

"He shares your table manners."

"Cool it Greves."

Finished they sat round the table, the maid taking away their bowls and coming back with the main course.

Cam cut at it clumsily, more tearing than slicing the meat, putting the knife down to switch the fork to her right hand. She shovelled in the chunks, hardly chewing, stabbing meat and vegetables, her lack of elegance surprising John. She finished and lit a cigarette.

"You want some desert?" Greves said.

She shook her head. "Some coffee, brandy would be good."

John ate his lamb, pushing the vegetables around the plate but avoiding actually eating them. She noticed and smiled but didn't say anything. He put his cutlery down and pushed the plate away.

"And you, John is it? Would you like some ice-cream?"

"Fuck off."

He reached across and took the cigarette packet, mashing one into his mouth and lighting it, desperate not to choke. She nodded in approval at him, pleased he had shown some fire, but she had to control this, she needed a way out of this country and most of all, her money back.

"So Greves." Breaking into the staring contest. "What's it going to cost me to get to France?"

"Both of you?"

"Yes."

"It's not going to be cheap Cam, the passport you wanted is going to be eighty on its own."

"That pounds?"

"Euros."

"And that's to the bone, full trace back?"

"I have a man in the Home Office, he will insert the necessary and remove the old, you'll need a new name."

Eighty Euros John thought, that seemed reasonable, but to give up his name, could he do it?

"Well John, you got a name you want to be?" Cam said.

"I, I don't know, I haven't thought about it, I have always been John."

"You better think quickly."

So this was it, a new name, living in a different country, his parents dead, just him now, and maybe Cam, but how long would she stay around? She had wanted rid of him before, he was useless to her, useless to anyone, what was the point?

"Pick any name you want." He said, drawing deeply on the cigarette.

"OK." He turned to Cam. "Yours is cheaper, just thirty, I can get you tickets for the train, that's another seven each, plus my commission, accommodation etc., call it two hundred."

She nodded. "Two hundred thousand."

"Yes, Euros."

"Take it out of what you owe me."

"I already have." He threw a charm necklace on to the table, she picked it up and ran her fingers over it.

"Mnemonic?"

"Yes."

"OK." She fastened it around her throat and looked at John. "Go with Greves, he's going to scan you and take some blood, set you up with a new ID."

"You ready kid?" Greves stood and walked towards a door opposite the one they had come in through.

"My name is John, not kid."

"Not for long."

Five

Detective Sergeant Nicholas Jenkins slammed the car door and grimaced at the scene in front of him. The blaze had been extinguished leaving a burnt out shell where the betting shop had been, the fire crew now checking the neighbouring properties for damage, a launderette on one side, a charity shop on the other, both evacuated. He nodded at the single police officer standing next to a line of tape keeping the curious back. Nick glanced at the notes on his Perse, forensics had been and gone in ten minutes, nothing useful had survived the burning, the witnesses conflicting in their testimony. Surprise at the station when he volunteered to take the case, not that he had a choice, he had been summoned there, reminded of who he was, who he owed, who owned him.

"D.S. Jenkins." He said to the uniform, held up his Perse flashing his warrant.

"Sir. P.C. Aberinkula." The woman gave him a smile, straightened her back.

"Anything here? Other than the obvious?"

"No sir, I arrived here fifteen minutes ago, was told to stand here and control the scene."

"Are you new Aberinkula?"

"Graduated last month sir."

"I see." He nodded. "Well, there's not much here for you to guard, I suggest you continue with your patrol."

"Sir?"

"Go on, it will be fine." He typed on his Perse. "I've signed it off. You can be on your way."

"I'd like to stay sir, my intention is to apply to CID as soon as I am able."

"Commendable, commendable." He frowned, he needed the woman to leave.

"However this isn't a good case for you to observe, I'm just going to run the licence plate and work from there, fairly routine. Pretty boring actually."

"Still."

"Still nothing." He made a shooing gesture. "Be on your way."

He watched her expression change, a brief flicker of annoyance quickly masked.

"Sir." She said. Pushed past a bystander and walked away. He watched her go, wishing he could leave as well, but he had been told to wait for his master like a good little doggie.

One of the signs in the betting shop window was still active, flickering odds on the Saturday games, he watched them change while he waited.

A limousine pulled up behind his car, engine idling. He approached it, opened the rear door and got in. He sank into the leather seat, keeping his feet back from a blanket that covered up something on the floor.

"You see it? What they did to my shop?"

"It looks bad Mr Marshall, terrible accident." Nick said.

"Accident! This was an attack on me."

"I don't see ..."

"They did my place on Marcus as well, three dead, money taken."

"Really? Do you want me to send some uniforms?"

"Uniforms! You stupid fuck, of course I don't want uniforms, I want you to find the cocksucker who did this and hand him to me."

"You think someone drove into the bookies on purpose?"

"How dense are you? Why have I only got idiots on my payroll?"

'Because it's only idiots who owe you money' Nick thought. He said. "You think Lennon's murder is related?"

"Lennon?"

"One of your collectors, worked the casino district, found dead in an alley near there."

"What the fuck? You're just telling me this now?"

"Just came in, looks amateur, someone spat in his face. Running the DNA, we'll have a name by the end of the day."

Marshall kicked the blanket which writhed and shrank back from the blow. Pretending he hadn't noticed Nick kept his gaze away from it.

"You find who is doing this and you bring them to me, do you understand?" Marshall said.

"I doubt they're connected, it's just a coincidence."

"Coincidence." Marshall shook his head. "That's why you work for me, not the other way round."

It had started out with a gambling debt too large for him to pay, Marshall had suggested another way to settle his account. It seemed easy at the time, lose some evidence and all was squared. The next slip and he was back in again, this time deeper, the thug with the iron bar, his arm on blocks ready to be shattered, Marshall coming in to the room, shaking his head, pained him to do this, but perhaps there was something else, Nick begging, saying yes, anything. Planting drugs in the lawyer's car, a life destroyed, but not his, he swore that was it but then he got a tip on the Cup Final, a sure thing, couldn't lose.

Except he did.

"We'll pick up Lennon's killer soon, the other stuff, well." He shrugged. "We haven't much to go on."

"Give me him for a few hours, I will find out who he's

working with."

"I don't think..."

"That's right, don't think, do as I say. Get out."

Nick started to speak, then thought better of it, nodded and got out of the car. He watched it pull from the kerb before returning to his own. He sat behind the wheel with his eyes closed, trying to regain his composure, trying to forget what had been under the blanket in the back of Marshall's car. He drew a deep breath, pushed the thoughts away, pulled out his Perse and logged the time, checked for updates on his cases. He watched the bookie's change, switched to his personal account and placed a bet, the odds too good to pass up.

Maya thought this was the nicest hotel she had ever been in, the marble foyer was clean and bright, freshly decorated, there were bunches of flowers, real flowers, everywhere. The staff were wearing uniforms and had pleasant expressions, the clientèle were well dressed, well behaved, they wouldn't be screaming at three in the morning or fighting on the balcony, throwing trash into the pool.

She said. "This is like in a Thread."

"Sit there." He said, pointing at one of the chairs and left her to go to the reception desk. She sank into the seat then rocked forward to take a sweet from a bowl on the table.

David Wallace watched the man walk over to him, formed a smile of polite greeting.

"Good afternoon Sir, how can I help you today?"

"I'd like a room, a twin, for five days."

"I'll just check if we have anything available."

"Nothing higher than the second floor, I have a thing about heights."

"Of course." The receptionist smiled at him. "Could I have your ID?"

"Here." He handed over his card, Wallace glanced at the

picture and tapped it to his screen.

"Thank you Mr Redentor." He slid the card back. "And your... friend?"

"She's not stopping."

"The room is the same price regardless of the number of occupants."

"Do I look like I care about money?"

He pulled out a stack of notes and placed them on the counter. Wallace stared at them, blinked.

"Of course not Mr Redentor."

"The room?"

Wallace removed several from the pile, slipped one in to his pocket.

"Number 248, the lift is on your right. Do you need a hand with your luggage?"

"Thanks, no, I will be fine."

He picked his bag up and headed to the lifts, passing Maya he gestured for her to follow him. They rode up in silence, he waved her out before him and they walked down the hall towards the room. He unlocked the door and ushered her in, closed it and attached the screamer.

Maya stood slack jawed staring at the room, the twin beds looked like doubles, a thick duvet on each, two large leather recliners in front of the Ent. She went into the bathroom; large tub and separate shower. Gold on everything.

"It meet with your approval?"

She jumped at his words.

"It's amazing."

"Well don't get too comfortable, we won't be here that long."

"Can I have a bath?"

"Sure, go for it."

"Thank you."

"I'm going to order room service – there anything you want?"

She hadn't thought about food, about how hungry she was.
"Yes, I'll have, do they have Gafutys?"
"I doubt it, but they will do a burger."
"Please, with cheese and bbq sauce."
"OK."
"And a Mr Fizzy."
"A Mr Fizzy?"
"Yes, it's a drink."
"I know it's a drink, it's for kids."
She pouted. "I like Mr Fizzy."
"OK, whatever."

He shoved a cigarette into his mouth and left the bathroom. She heard him talking, ordering the food.

Maya ran the bath, pouring in the lotions that she found on the side, they foamed up colouring the water and filling the air with scent. She stripped and eased in, the water almost too hot to bear, submerging until she was in up to her neck, the heat making her light headed, drowsy, easing the Grindache. She had three shots left but then what would she do? He cared so little for the money it would be easy to take some and buy more. If she could get away, she would need an excuse. Should she come back though? Why hadn't she run already? He had given her enough chances, did she want to stay with him? Did he mean it, that he would teach her to steal, to kill? Why didn't he want to fuck her? Was he gay? Maybe that was it, but the way he had looked at her, the desire on his face, that wasn't the way a queer would look at her.

He sat in one of the chairs, his attention flitting from the hallway door to the bathroom one. What was he doing with her? Why had she stuck around? He had given her enough opportunities to leave, she could have taken the money at any time. What did she want? Was he serious about training her? Could she handle it? She was only a kid but then he hadn't been much older when he had killed his first man. That had been an accident, two weeks in the box as punishment, baking in the Arizonan sun. Then his first deliberate murder, a car bomb packed with ball bearings and nails parked on a busy street. Body parts scattered and mashed, the wail of sirens breaking the silence after the explosion. Watching the carnage from a balcony his instructor had patted him approvingly on the back. Screams from the survivors beginning to build, his knees buckling, vomit spraying from his lips as the enormity of what he had done sank in. Another week in the box for showing weakness, curled up in his soiled clothes, eyes pressed closed trying to forget the images burnt in to his memory. Later, when he told Cam about the bomb she had shaken her head, 'inelegant' she had said but he had seen her do far worse.

Human life meant little to her, except her own.

And his.

In the end she had shown she loved him, sacrificed herself for him. He had left her bleeding to death, turned his back and ran.

The knock at the door broke his reverie, he brushed the tears from his face and deactivated the screamer, carelessly opening it without checking the screen.

"Room Service Sir."

He stood aside and waited for the trolley to be wheeled in, the cloches removed to show the food. He glanced at the pad they presented him to thumb and instead handed over a couple of notes.

"Thanks."

"Thank you Sir." The waiter grinned, pleased with the substantial tip. He closed the door after them and reactivated the screamer.

"Maya! Your food is here."

He picked up a burger and a bottle of beer, sat back in the chair, woke the Ent up.

"Local news. Text summary." He said, scanned through the

headlines, nothing on Lennon, but the fire had made an article, 'Car drives into betting shop, three people injured.'

He took a swig of beer. "Maya!"

"I'm here."

She said, coming out of the bathroom wearing a thick white robe with her hair tied up in a towel turban. She grabbed her plate and sat in the chair next to his, bit in to the burger, she couldn't remember the last time she ate, Grind didn't suppress your appetite but it could distract you from the hunger. She pushed the straw in to the Mr Fizzy carton and slurped from it. She licked the sauce from her fingers, felt his eyes on her, she looked at him and emphasised the sucking, pushing each one into her mouth and slowly out. Frustrated and embarrassed he turned from her back to the Ent.

She finished her food, drained the carton, stood and put them both back on the trolley.

"Did you mean it?" She said.

"Huh?"

"What you said about training me?"

He waved the Ent to standby, rubbed his face with his hands and said. "Yeah, why not?"

He unzipped his bag, tipping the contents out on to the floor and pushing the cash to one side with little concern. She dropped to her knees and began scooping it up, sorting it into bundles and stacking it. He ignored her, picked up a machine pistol and ejected the magazine, counting the number of rounds left; half a clip. He replaced it with a full one and then checked the other pistol; three cartridges. He sprang them free with his thumb and added them to the half clip, returned that and the empty one to the bag. He used one of the remaining mags to reload the pistol leaving him with four spare. He took the automatic from its shoulder holster and ejected the clip, two cartridges left but he had a box of 9mm for that. He racked the slide ejecting the round from the breech.

"Maya, leave the money."

She stopped counting and looked up, he handed her the gun grip first. She took it, surprised at its weight, he held out the magazine.

"Slide it in."

She did as instructed, puzzled when it jammed halfway.

"No, the bullets face forward."

Flustered, she reversed it and this time the magazine clicked home.

"Now, chamber a round."

She looked puzzled, he took the gun back and showed her.

"You try."

She repeated his action, jumping when a cartridge shot out of the breech.

"Again."

Another round spat out.

"Again."

Nothing happened.

"Eject the clip." He pointed at the release button, which she pressed, dropping the magazine free.

He picked it up and pushed the rounds back in.

"Now, release the safety." Indicating the switch above the trigger. She pushed it up to reveal a red dot.

"Pull the trigger."

She did so, it was harder than she imagined it would be.

"Put the safety back on."

He handed her the clip.

"Insert the magazine and chamber a round."

She pushed it back in and racked it.

"OK. Shall I release the safety?"

"No, unless you want us kicked out of the hotel."

He smiled at her, held out his hand for the gun. She smiled back at him leaning forward to give him it, letting the robe drop open. He coloured and looked away.

She pouted. "I don't understand, don't you want me?"

"I would've thought you'd want a break from fucking."

She scowled, and let the gun drop, he grabbed it out of the air.

He could feel his cock stiffening, why not fuck her? It wasn't that she was an innocent to be protected, she was a whore, she must have done anything he could imagine, more. So why didn't he?

She slumped back in her chair.

"Can I have the Ent on?" She said.

"Sure, why not." He scooped his stuff back in to the bag and zipped it up. Maya flicked through channels, he lit a cigarette, finished his beer.

"I need to do some reconnaissance." He said.

She looked away from the Ent. "Can I come?"

"It could be dangerous."

"I thought you wanted to teach me to do what you do."

Did he? He had offered her the opportunity, but it was a stupid idea, she wasn't a killer, wasn't a thief. But then he hadn't been when he first met Cam. He had just been a boy, not much older than Maya was now.

"You'll need some clothes." He gestured at the Ent. "Shopping channel, women's, casual evening."

She giggled, dropped her robe and stood on the dais, hand gestures flicking through the items overlaid on her body, posing for him.

"You like this one?"

"Get what you want, not too showy, what a young girl would wear out on a date."

"A first date?" She said.

"I'm going to get a shower."

He left her to choose, pushing the bathroom door closed and removed his jacket, a gift from Cam, bullet resistant, with a knife snagging lining, it had protected him from the shotgun pellets but not the force of the blast and his shoulder was beginning to purple and stiffen. He stripped and got into the cubicle, lathered and rinsed, his eye on the door. He hadn't locked it, did he want her to come in? He got out and dried off, wrapping the towel around his waist. He rubbed his fingers together checking the slight oiliness that meant the thingloves were still intact. He would need to use the shredder again, the can was in his bag in the other room. He picked his clothes up and opened the door.

She turned at the sound, stared at his body, lean and hard, a swirl of words across his chest and curling round his waist.

"What does it say?"

He realised she was talking about his tattoo. "Life song."

"Life song?"

"A record of my life, accomplishments and deeds."

"It's not very long."

"There's still time." He hoped. "You ordered something?"

"Yes, will be here in the hour."

"Good."

He crouched by the bag and rummaged for the can of shredder, he stood, awkward wondering if he should go back in to the bathroom, shrugged and let the towel drop. He sprayed himself and then beckoned to her.

"What is it?"

"Shredder, destroys DNA."

"Isn't that dangerous?"

"Moderately, means you don't leave any evidence, worth the cost."

She removed her robe, turned round allowing him to spray her, faced him again and touched the chain wrapped around his wrist, jangling the tokens hanging from it.

"What are those?"

"Supposed to be lucky charms."

"Do they work?"

"Not so far they haven't."

She smiled and stroked his cock. "And how about this, does it work?"

"Maya."

"You don't like it?"

"No, I."

"It looks like you like it."

She gripped him. Why was he resisting her? He made no attempt to remove her hand, letting the pleasure build. Why was he resisting her? Disloyalty to Cam? It felt like a betrayal, she had sacrificed herself for him, he couldn't do it. He thought back to when he had last seen her, lying broken and bloody on the ground, this wasn't right.

"I'm sorry."

He pulled away from her, bent to get some clothes out of the bag. She stood, arms dropped to her sides, feeling helpless. If he didn't want her then he would get tired of her, kill her or dump her on the street, dead either way. She picked her robe up and put it on.

"Then what?" She said.

"After your clothes arrive we'll go out."

"OK." Frustrated she dropped back in to her chair, switched the Ent to a gossip channel and focused on it.

He opened another beer, and sat watching her as much as the Ent. The celebrities on it meant nothing to him, too localised and besides he had had little opportunity for popular culture in the last 8 years.

"Who's that?" He nodded at the dais where a man was singing in a lazy vocal style, words mumbled and flowing together.

"Hendo – he's the best."

"Sounds terrible."

"What do you like?" She sat up and leant towards him. "We can watch something else."

"Nothing I like will be on, this is fine."
"Where are you from?"
"Huh?"
"Your accent, you talk like someone off the Threads."
"Do I?"
"Yes, where are you from."
"It doesn't matter, it's where you're going that counts."
"And where are you going?"
"Huh?"
"Where are you going?"
"I, I don't know." He waved his hands. "I don't really have a plan."
"You say some strange stuff."
"I guess."
"You guess?" She tsked and he thought of Cam.
"Yeah, I guess."
Relieved when the door chimed.
"That'll be my stuff!" She jumped and ran for the door.
"Maya, stop!" He ran past her to deactivate the screamer.

Minus Six

Back at the garage, John got in to the passenger seat, waited for Greves to start the car. They drove out on to the street, the gate swinging shut behind them.

Breaking the silence, Greves said. "So how long have you known Cam?"

"Long enough."

Greves laughed. "Yes, you've certainly picked up her tacitness. How about her disdain for technology?"

"Huh?"

"I take it you have a Perse?"

"Oh yeah." John pulled it out and showed it to him.

"Good, you switched it off, I was going to tell you to do that. Wouldn't be wise to trace this route. You would be best to dump it anyway."

"It's got my music on, photos."

"Photos? Not a good idea to keep those."

"But."

"When you get your ID, buy a new one, transfer what you want over and trash that one. Don't turn it back on till you get out of the country though."

"I will." John said, confused at this turn in conversation. "Thanks."

"Once you're out of my house it's no matter to me what you do, no skin off my nose if you get caught cos of an old picture of your mum."

At the mention of her John felt the tears well up again, he rubbed his eyes and looked out the window. They paused at an intersection, waiting for the lights to change, Greves turning left onto Mortimer Street.

"Where is this place, is it far?" John said.

"Not that far, still in the controlled zone, it's in the Home Office, you know what that is?"

"Yeah, part of the old government, does visas and stuff."

"Yes, even though the counties are autonomous they are still united on national matters and have representatives that serve here in the old capital."

"Oh." John said, not appreciating the history lesson.

"Not interested?"

"I've read about it, I know how it works." He said, not wanting to explain he had covered it that term in school. Greves had been teasing him about his youth as it was, he would have a field day knowing that John hadn't graduated.

"Right."

They drove through the city, Greves cutting down side streets and across others, eventually turning off to stop in front of a barrier. He dialled a number on his Perse, hanging up without speaking, the gate in front of them rolled open and they drove in, parking in one of the free spaces.

"Here we are." He said, getting out. John followed him, having to run to catch the man before he reached a nondescript door in the side of the building. It opened, a young woman standing on the threshold, she nodded to Greves and beckoned them in. She closed the door behind them, thumbed it locked. They stood in a grey painted corridor, heavy old cast iron radiators on the walls under single glazed windows, the putty round their edges dried and peeling away. The parquet flooring gleamed under the patina from centuries of footsteps.

"Thank you, I do appreciate this." Greves said.

She nodded. "Full scan?"

"Yes, and black holing."

"Expensive."

He handed her a card which she slipped into her pocket.

"Follow me."

She led them along the corridor and down a flight of stairs at the end, stopping in front of a door with a sign saying 'Processing Centre' above it. She thumbed it open, holding it for them to pass in to a room painted white, clinically clean, the furniture in it sparse and utilitarian; a desk with a monitor on it, an examination bed with pull down disposable sheets and an upright scanner in the corner.

"This won't take long, just step into the scanner, place your hands flat on the wall and stare at the X." The woman said.

John hesitated, wondering if it was too late to back out.

"Come on kid." Greves said, causing the boy to bristle.

"Step in to the scanner."

Concentrating on the screen the woman ignored the interplay between them.

Inside John noticed hand outlines on one wall, he pressed his palms on them and stared at the X marked above them.

"OK, come out." She tapped out responses on a screen. "New name?"

"Allow me." Greves typed it in, she glanced at it and grunted, touched a confirmation prompt.

"You done?" John said, surprised at how quick it had been, Greves was charging eighty thousand Euros for two minutes work!

"Not yet, still need a sample, Cam wanted your ID to be black holed as well."

"Black holed?"

"Someone scans your ID and they get a clean hit, no warrants, no record. Strange request really, you killed someone, left your scazz on em?"

"No, I, I haven't killed anyone."

Greves shook his head. "Doesn't matter to me, she's paying for it."

The woman handed John a swab. "Run this inside your cheek."

He scraped it inside his mouth and handed it back, she dropped it into a reader and looked satisfied at the green light. More confirmations and a long string of digits then she said. "It's done."

"I have another ID, I want, surface detail only." Greves handed her a datapos.

"OK, they will be ready in a minute." She said, passing it over a scanner and offering him it back, he shook his head and she dropped it into the secure bin.

"That's it then? That's all there is to getting a new ID?" John said.

"It's not complicated to print an ID, the issue is getting the information into the database. The government restricts access to it, that's where the expense lies. If you have access you can put anything you want in there, change anything, remove anything. That's what you're, or rather Cam is paying for."

"There you go, as requested." The woman said holding out a couple of ID cards.

Greves pocketed them. "Thank you." He gave a brief smile. "Right we're done here."

The woman let them back out the building, closing the door without saying goodbye.

"Such a sullen person." Greves said. "But excellent at her job."

"How did you find her?"

"Ah, after my secrets are you?" Greves tapped his nose.

"No, just wondered."

"It's the nature of my business, knowing which hands to grease and which ones to bite."

"Oh."

Greves unlocked the car, motioned for John to get in.

"Perhaps if you had something of interest to trade then I would be willing to tell you."

"I don't really care." John looked down at his hands, noticed the yellow tinge on the edge of his forefinger and rubbed at it.

"Smoking." Greves said, he started the engine and backed them out of the spot, turning the car to pass out through the gate.

"Huh?"

"Like Cam, you smoke, a filthy habit."

"I guess it is."

"Dangerous too."

"Why? There's a cure for cancer."

Greves shook his head. "You don't slice your hand off because you know they can stitch it back on."

"Whatever." He wished he had brought a pack with him though he wasn't sure he would have been brave enough to light one. "We nearly back?"

"Yes, I noticed how close you two were, you must be keen to get back in to her... arms."

John fumed, unsure how to respond, in the end decided not to speak, not give this man any more chances to goad him. He didn't like the way Greves was baiting him, always with the jibes, what was his problem? Cam was paying him enough – two hundred thousand – he couldn't believe it! She'd spent it without blinking. And what had he said, the money he'd laundered for her – ten million pounds! Wow, he couldn't even imagine that amount of money. Had she stolen it from Marshall? Is that why he wanted her so bad? He could understand him torturing her for that, wondered what lengths the man would go to get it back.

Could he ever go home?

The drive continued in silence, John staring out the window

at the city streets passing by.

London!

A place he had always dreamt of visiting, and he was on the residents side as well.

It didn't look much like he had imagined, didn't look much different from his home town. But then, what had he been expecting, flying cars and robots? It was mid-afternoon and a few people were walking, taking advantage of the good weather, they seemed to be better dressed than back home, the cars they passed more expensive, even some he had only seen before on Cool Rides.

When they pulled into the parking space he got out and strode towards the lift, realised he had to wait for Greves to authorise them, and impatiently waited for the man to catch up, tried to ignore the smug expression on his face.

He exited first, heading to the Ent room where Cam was sat on a couch, her feet up on an ottoman, her eyes closed.

"Cam?"

She opened them and sat up, stretched, stifled a yawn.

"All done?" She said, picked a pack of cigarettes off a side table and lit one. John nodded and sat down next to her.

Greves walked in to the room, held out the IDs to her, she took them, glanced at hers, then scowled at John's.

"This a joke?"

"I thought it appropriate, after all he's no longer using it."

She passed the card to John, he read the name but it meant nothing to him.

"It's done now." She said. "When is the train?"

Greves checked his Perse. "I booked you on the six thirty this evening."

"Fine, wake us when it's time to go." She stood up, tucked her ID in to the cigarette pack and left the room. "John."

Greves grinned at him. "Better do what you're told."

John glared back, tried to think of a witty reply, failed and

Joe Mansour

ran to catch her up

Greves dropped them at St Pancras station, pulling into the loading zone at the front, his residents pass enough to keep the wardens away.

"Service with a smile." He said, his face twisted into something resembling one.

"Thanks Greves, next time I'm in London yes?"

"Of course Cam, my home is always open to you."

He looked in the rear view mirror. "And you of course, if you're still around."

"Um, thanks." John got out the back and waited for her. She pushed her door shut and lit a cigarette, held the pack out to him. He took one and the lighter, watched Greves pull away.

"We need to get out of this fucking country." She walked into the station.

This fucking country she called it, his home, would he ever see it again?

He followed her in, stopping in the atrium to look around. A bustle of people moving about, announcements blaring, signs updating, armed police on watch at the barriers. He lost sight of Cam, began to panic, what would he do if he couldn't find her? Spotted her walking to the area marked 'International Travel Only' and ran over to her.

"Cam." He said.

"Not at the moment."

She touched her ID to a turnstile allowing her to pass into the scanner and then out into the dead man's zone, no longer on UK soil, with a walk of twenty metres to the immigration booth for the U.E.C.

"Get a move on." She said, waved at him to follow her.

John tapped his card on the turnstile and waited for the sirens to start wailing.

"Stop fucking around, these guards are arseholes, don't piss them off." She said.

He pushed on the barrier, felt it give allowing him in to the scanner, a brief buzz, a green light and he stepped out.

"About time." She said, grabbing him by the elbow and pulling him along.

At the other end of the corridor a couple of Eurocops waited, dressed head to foot in armour, mirrored visors reflecting their image back to them.

"ID." One said, to his left the other pointed a machine gun in their direction. Cam and John held up their cards, a laser flickered over their surface followed by

"Go through."

"Right." Cam said to John. "The platform's over there."

This wasn't like the trains he was used to. For a start, none of the windows were smashed and the seats weren't ripped. Their tickets secured them a cabin, four seats with a table in the middle. Cam sat down and closed her eyes, he took the seat next to her, wondered if he should have picked the one opposite.

"Cam?"

"Huh?" She looked at him, what did he want now?

"What will we do in France?"

"When we get to Paris?"

"Yes."

"I was thinking I'd put you in a school. You know, a boarding one?"

"A boarding school - like Harry Potter?"

"Could be, I don't know who he is."

"He's a wizard."

"A wizard?"

"Everyone knows who Harry Potter is."

"I don't have much time for wizards."

"That's besides the point, what I meant is, you want me to

go to a boarding school?"

"What else could I do with you?"

"I could come with you."

"No."

"Why not?"

"My life, I don't have, look my life is haphazard, I don't have time for babysitting."

"Babysitting! I'm not a baby."

"You know what I mean." She pulled out a pack and lit a cigarette. "You must have an idea what I do."

"Yes, you steal from people."

"Well, sometimes, also I remove people's problems, or a country's problems for that matter."

"What does that mean?"

"It means I don't have time for tourists, for someone hanging around that could get me killed."

"I could help."

"Help?" She snorted. "How could you help me?"

"I don't know, surely it's better to have someone?"

"Not if it means they get me killed."

"You could teach me."

"I don't have time."

"Still."

"Leave it John, I need to get focused, we will talk when I know what's going on."

Trying to keep the petulant look off his face he stared out the window. She closed her eyes, heard him rustling, caught him reaching for the cigarettes. She smiled and pushed them over.

"Cam?"

"Yes?"

"How long till we get to France?"

The train sped through the countryside, John stared out of

the window amazed at their speed, 300kph according to the display. Cam slept, her head leaning on the glass. He glanced at her face, thought back to earlier, to the sex, they had done it several times, he could feel himself getting hard remembering it.

She wanted to put him in a boarding school, thought he was a kid but she had still fucked him, what did that say about her? Of course she had been through a lot, he paled at the thought of Marshall's cellar, she might not be acting normally, though he wondered what normal was in her case. Did she even think that deeply about what she did or was it just something to do?

Cam ceased the chant, an old trick to keep distracted from the pain preventing her from sleeping, and opened her eyes. The display gave a countdown to Paris, less than 20 minutes till they arrived. Now in France, the tunnel long behind them, at last she could relax, at least for a while. John was staring out at the fields, was he serious about wanting to come with her or was he just scared to be alone? Well who wasn't? She had been on her own a while now, since Holt, she hadn't wanted to get that involved again, not with someone she worked with, who might betray her, who did betray her. But this boy had no past agenda, no baggage, she could make him whatever she wanted. They had got the fucking out of the way, one less issue to deal with; unresolved sexual tension. She smiled and lit a cigarette. John heard the sound and looked over, noticed her smile and returned it. She squinted and blew smoke, watched the readout click down until they pulled into Gard du Nord.

"We'll eat." She said, customs a mere formality that they passed through with a wave of their IDs. Outside the station she stopped at one of the cafés clustered around it, picked a table on the pavement and waved a waiter over.

"What do you want?" She asked John.

"Uh." He stared at the menu unable to read it. "Do they do burgers?"

"I imagine so." She lit a cigarette and said to the waiter.

"<A burger, the pork with lentils and two beers.>"

"<Certainly.>" He typed the order on his Perse, gave a half smile and went in to the café to get the drinks.

"You speak French?" John said.

"Advantage of being from a former colony."

"Uh?"

"You learn a few languages. Don't you speak it?"

"No."

"At school, you telling me they don't teach you a language? Any language?"

"We had the option, I picked biology instead."

"That do you any good?"

"I dunno, I guess."

She shook her head, tapped ash on the ground. The waiter placed the beers in front of them, she held her hand out stopping John from showing his ID.

"What do we do now?" He said.

She sipped her beer. What to do now? The job was done, she was away and Marshall could be forgotten. On to the next one, but first she had to sort her finger out. And John as well. She sighed, stared at him waiting for her to speak. Was he serious about coming with her? Could she do that to him, make him into a thief, a killer? Better to go with the original plan and put him in a school. He would thank her later.

"Cam?"

"I'm thinking about it."

"You're thinking about dumping me."

"Look John." She leant forward, touched the back of his hand. "You don't want to stay with me, my life, it's not easy."

"I want you to teach me."

"Why?"

"So that I can go back and kill Marshall." His face screwed up trying to hold back tears.

Oh, so that was it, revenge.

"Quickest way to die John, you should leave it and move on."

"Move on!"

He clenched the edge of the table to stop from shaking.

"He killed my parents!"

"OK, keep it down."

She held one of his hands, felt the tension in it.

"Calm down, just calm down, we'll talk about this again, let's just eat. We need to go to the bank then a hotel, then we will talk about it, but for now, leave it."

He closed his eyes, tried to get control, tried to stop the shaking and the tears that were leaking through the lids. He needed her to train him, to show him how to kill, he needed this, not some boarding school in France, some made up life to go with his made up name. He swore he would find a way to become John McPhereson again, swore that he would go back and kill Marshall, he would make him pay. But for now he had to do what she said, so she wouldn't leave him. He steeled himself and opened his eyes.

"OK." He said, reached for the pack and took out a cigarette.

"OK." She leant back, picked up her glass, drank, closed her eyes positioning herself in the moment, savouring it.

"Does it still hurt?"

"What?"

"Your finger." He nodded at it. "Does it hurt still?"

"Of course it does."

"You don't seem bothered by it."

"There are techniques you can use to isolate pain, separate it off and control it."

"So it doesn't hurt?"

"It still hurts, I just don't let it control me."

"Can you teach me that?"

"Who said I was going to teach you anything."

"Cam."

She smiled and his heart thumped a beat through his chest, thoughts swirling back to earlier on when they had been in bed, when they were having sex, would they again? It had been incredible, better than he had imagined or hoped. He couldn't leave her, go back to a normal life, not after this.

"Eat your food." She said as the waiter placed it in front of him. He eyed the burger with suspicion, the meat an off putting pink rather than the grey he was accustomed to. Relieved that they provided ketchup he slathered it on his food and took a bite.

"It's good." He said, picking up some chips.

"I understand they're famed for the burgers here."

She scooped up the lentils with her fork, tearing at the meat with the tines and shovelling it in to her mouth.

"Really?"

She shook her head and went back to eating. He decided that it was a joke, or her attempt at one, it would be something to puzzle out if she agreed to teach him, to try and understand her sense of humour, maybe even make her laugh.

They finished and she paid with a card Greves had sold her.

"<Where's the nearest bank?>" She asked the waiter.

"<There is a cash machine on this street madame.>"

She bridled at the madame, said. "<I need a bank, not a machine.>"

"<In that case there is one on the corner of Italian boulevard where it meets Helder street.>"

"<Thanks.>"

She stood up, dropping her napkin on the table.

"Where we going?" He said, catching her up and dropping in to step.

"To the bank. If you see a cab stick your hand out."

"There's a cash machine over there." He pointed.

"They use DNA, and I don't have any on hand."

"Huh?"

She stopped.

"When you're in my business then you don't want to leave your DNA lying around. Petty thieves shave their heads, scrub their bodies prior to a job. But if you want something more effective you use a shredder."

"A shredder?"

"It's a chemical, it destroys your DNA, you spray it on."

"That sounds dangerous."

"There're risks to everything, better than being caught by a stray skin cell. Your body is the star witness for the prosecution."

"Greves said I had been black holed."

"Yes, but that was more of a reset."

"What about fingerprints?"

"Thingloves." She stroked his face with her hand, the touch had a light oiliness that had felt so good when she was gripping his cock. "You can wear them for days, weeks even. Until they become too frayed and you have to replace them."

"I see, so you can't use a cash machine."

"No, we need to go to a bank, get my money the old fashioned way."

"OK, is it far?"

She shook her head and walked down the road, another cigarette in her mouth. He watched her stride away admiring her arse, thinking back to the afternoon, no way was he going to a boarding school. John scurried after her, falling in besides her and asked for a cigarette.

"You need to buy your own."

"I don't have any money."

"Need to get some then don't you?"

"How?"

"Is that my problem?"

"Cam."

"Don't Cam me, don't beg, we make our way through life

alone, dependent on no one but ourselves."

"Sounds lonely."

She laughed. "Yes, it can be."

"Take me with you Cam, teach me."

She handed over the pack. "I wouldn't be doing you a favour, this life is pain, there is little reward to it."

"What is life without pain?"

"Schopenhauer!"

"Yes, we did him in general studies."

"School." She stopped and turned to him.

"John, you're so young, you don't want this life, it will destroy you."

He lit a cigarette, breathed the smoke in, held it and then let it flow from his nose, no choking cough, he began to see the point.

"Cam, I have nothing but this, it's all gone, my parents are dead. Marshall took everything I had."

"I won't help you kill him, I'm done with that place, that county."

"Just train me, that's all."

"Let me think about it." She continued down the street. When his parents said that it meant no. If she wasn't going to teach him then what would he do? He caught up with her.

"OK." He said.

"Better." She smiled at him, lit a cigarette from the stub of the last.

"We get some money, sort out my finger, then a hotel, get the fucking day back in order. Then we take stock, plan our next move."

Our next move, hope filled him, had she decided to take him with her? And if she had, then was it really what he wanted. No time to be having second thoughts. If she put him in a school then it was all over, he wasn't equipped to exact his revenge, he needed her. More than that though, he wanted her, it wasn't love but it was something, something he hadn't experienced before.

Six

He felt naked without a weapon, Cam would have chided him for feeling that way. You used what was to hand, over reliance on a gun, or a knife, made you sloppy, made you weak if you were deprived of it. 'Your body is a weapon' she had said, which sounded like some sort of Gongfu shit. The casino had detectors on the door, he wouldn't get in with one, be made straight away. Besides this was just a recce, get the lay of the land, work out a course of action, he didn't expect trouble, wouldn't start any.

Maya walked beside him, feeling strange to be so over dressed, so modestly dressed. She was nervous, it felt like she was on a date, or what she imagined a date to be like, she reached over to grab his hand, pleased when he returned the grip.

"Uh Chris?"

"Yes?"

"Will we need ID to, you know, go in to the casino?"

He stopped. "Don't you have ID?"

"No."

"Right." Of course he should have asked. He lit a cigarette, stared at her.

"Chris?"

"I thought you were sixteen?"

"I am." She bit her bottom lip.

"Why don't you have a card?"

"I didn't apply for one." Living on the outskirts of regular society she had little interaction with it other than the police and they had no problem identifying her.

He looked over at the casino, a windowless cube dominating the skyline, the buildings on each side dwarfed by it. Two DoorSec stood at the entrance checking people as they went in.

"Chris?"

He pointed at a restaurant, 'Sticky Fingers Smokehouse', faux wood cabin front, a neon cowgirl with sauce dripping from her chin flashing above it.

"We're here now." He said. "Might as well eat."

He asked for a booth and they were led down the rows of tables to one at the back, Maya got in first, sliding across the leatherette seat to let him sit next to her.

"This is nice." She said.

He looked at the faded décor, tapped a cigarette from the pack and scowled at a 'no smoking' sign.

"You don't eat out much?" He said.

"No." She picked up her menu, scrolled through it marvelling at the choices. "Usually just a burger or chips from a take-out, did get taken to a VMD once by a John who was sweet on me."

"Yeah, what happened to him?"

"Dunno." She shrugged. "Never saw him after I turned thirteen."

"Christ."

"He was nice to me."

Not knowing how to respond, he looked at his menu, selected ribs and a T-bone; rare, a bottle of Tencher.

"You ordered?" He said.

She looked at the menu unsure what to have, picked the chilli poppers for starters, read the mains wondering what they were, felt his impatience and picked the most expensive; a fillet, panicked at the slider and left it at the middle, accepted the default sides, added a rum and coke. They returned the menus to the rack in the centre of the table propped between sauce bottles labelled with outlandish promises.

He tapped the cigarette on the pack, looked round the room.

Nervous, she watched him, he seemed on edge, restless, his fingers twirling the cigarette.

"So, tell me about yourself?" She said.

"Huh?" He turned back to her.

"I don't know anything about you."

"It's hardly the time for this."

"It's so the time, isn't that what you do on a date?"

"This isn't a date."

"Isn't it? Then why are we here?"

"I don't know." He really wanted a cigarette now, he pushed one between his lips and stood up.

"Wait here, I'll be back in a minute."

"Can't I come?"

"No."

Outside he lit up, sucking the smoke deep into his lungs, took the opportunity to look around. The casino was a fortress, no windows, reinforced doors. Bollards on the pavement to prevent a ram raid. Nothing came to mind other than a suicide run, he might as well strike it off, he would have to attack Marshall some other way. Cam had been right, it was stupid. He should just hunt Marshall down, put a bullet in his brain. He would be on his guard now, but still vulnerable to a sniper, easy if he could get a rifle. But no satisfaction, Marshall would die without knowing why, wouldn't get time to know, he wanted to look into the man's eyes, tell him the reason before he plunged the knife in. More foolishness, Cam had always laughed at the movies when the killer paused to explain their actions, she had said 'Don't take your eye off the game, shoot him first then explain after'. She was all business, nothing got in her way, no remorse, no fear, no compromise, her intent pure steel, her focus absolute. He had been her weak point, her flaw, if it hadn't been for him...

He flung the cigarette down, ground it out with his heel.

Waiting for Chris to come back, Maya toyed with her starter, the poppers were good, a nice spicy kick. She saw him walking towards the booth, her smile faltering at the angry expression on his face.

"Something the matter?" She said.

He slid in to the booth, his leg pressed against hers, shifted back to increase the distance.

"This was a bad idea." He said.

"Coming here?"

"The whole thing."

She looked puzzled, wondering if he meant the meal or something more. She chewed another popper, drained her drink and ordered a fresh one.

He picked a rib up and gnawed at the bone not really hungry after the burger, dropped it back on the plate with half the meat remaining on it, wiped his hands on a napkin. A waiter placed her drink down, she gulped half of it, tried not to think about the three shots of Grind in her new leather purse. How was she going to do another hit without him finding out? She could go a couple of days between, but knowing she had them made it so difficult to resist.

He swigged from his bottle, rolled it in his hands picking at the label.

"What do you want to know?" He said.

"Huh?" She looked up from her food.

"You said 'tell me about yourself?'."

"Oh yeah." She finished her second drink and pressed for a refill.

"So what do you want to know?"

The steaks arrived giving her time to think, she picked up an onion ring and crunched through the batter.

"These are good, you want one?"

"I'm fine with this, thanks." He cut into his steak, stabbed the piece onto a chip and chewed it.

"OK." She said. "What's your favourite Thread?"

He frowned, thinking.

"I don't really watch them, haven't in years, used to like 'Mento and the Ornatons', that still running?"

She shook her head. "I've never heard of it."

"Oh, well, then, nothing really, um, how about you?"

She smiled, thinking of the times when she had been allowed to watch an Ent, usually in between working they were stuck in a room, the floor covered in mattresses, girls and the occasional boy laying about, strung out on whatever they could get their hands on, music or a Thread playing in the background. Watching them had made her dream of a better life, an escape from her harsh reality.

"I really like 'Daisy's Life in the Moment' and Thorsten's shows are good."

"I don't know them." He finished his beer, tapped a finger on the cigarette pack.

She cut in to her steak, blinked at the blood oozing out and pushed the meat to one side of her plate.

She chewed her lip, tried to think of more questions to ask him.

"What about music, what do you like?"

"You won't have heard of it."

"I might."

"You won't."

"Fine." She ate another onion ring.

He put his cutlery down.

"You not going to eat that?" He indicated the fillet on her plate.

"Uh, no, not that hungry really." She had ordered without

knowing what it was, now faced with the reality she was reluctant to eat the pink flesh.

"OK." He pressed the bill icon, fed cash in to the slot, ignored the change, and slid out of the booth. She wobbled after him, woozy from the booze and caught him at the door, slipping her hand into his. He shook her off, lighting a cigarette as he exited.

"Can I have one?" She said.

"You should be buying your own."

"I don't have any money. How about a blow job?"

He blushed and handed her the pack. "We'll talk about it later."

"Where we going?"

"Back to the hotel."

"Why?"

"We're done here."

"And back at the hotel?"

He stopped. "What?"

"What'll we do there?" Half smile, she blew out smoke, touched her lips.

"I don't know, what do you want to do?"

She ran her finger down the front of his jacket. "We can do whatever you want."

"Right." He took her hand, moved it away. "What do you want?"

She shrugged. "I don't know, I've never been asked before."

"How about I teach you how to look after yourself?"

"Look after myself?"

"Yeah, you know, self defence."

"Hi-YA!"

She jumped and waved her arms around, kicked out a leg.

"What are you doing?"

"Karate, like on the Threads."

He laughed. "That's what it is is it?"

"Yes, now prepare to be defeated!"

She leapt at him flailing her arms, he dodged them and straight punched her to the chin. She reeled back holding her face.

"Ow! What did you do that for? I was only messing."

"I don't fight for fun." He grabbed her arm and started walking, she shook him off, stood with her hands on her hips glaring at him.

"Come on." He said.

"Why should I!"

Conscious of the casino DoorSec watching them he said.

"Maya, I don't have time for this."

"Time for what! You don't even know what you're going to do, all this talk about Marshall…"

He strode back to her and slapped her face. "Be quiet."

"Oi mate, what do you think you're playing at?" One of the guards walked towards them.

"Fuck off, this has nothing to do with you."

"Think you're big, hitting a woman, why don't you try it on me big man?"

Jason was tired of these clowns, losing their money and taking it out on their girlfriends or wives. She looked too young for him, not much older than his daughter Katie, she shouldn't be out at this time of night. She looked drunk as well, if he caught Katie drinking then she would get a slap, but only to warn her, to protect her, not like this guy here, he needed a slap as well, teach him that hitting a woman was wrong.

"Just fuck off right?"

"I'm OK." Maya sniffed. "It's OK, really."

"I think you're owed an apology, isn't that right mate – you need to apologise."Jason said, leaning in close.

He flicked his cigarette at Jason's face, kicked out, striking the bouncer's knee, followed it up with a hook to the ribs and, as Jason collapsed to the floor, he kicked him again, hard heel to the chest. He dropped beside him and punched him in the face, heard a noise and looked up, the other guard had run over and aimed a kick at him, he pushed it to the side and jabbed upwards into their balls, then hooked out their other leg crashing them to the ground, their head striking the pavement.

He stood back up, checked the area for threats, decided it was time to move on.

"You coming?" He said to Maya, not waiting for a reply he walked away heading for the hotel. Stunned by the rapid violence Maya looked down at the groaning men on the ground, the image of Lennon in her mind, horrified by the thought of what he might have done if he'd been armed!

She muttered an apology to them and ran off after him.

Back in the hotel he dropped into one of the chairs, another cigarette lit and hanging from his mouth. She opened the minibar, passed him a beer and took one for herself.

He nodded his thanks, twisted the cap off and drank, blew smoke from his nose. She sipped hers, thought of the Grind, tried to distract herself.

"You smoke a lot."

"I smoke enough."

"What does that mean?"

"It doesn't mean anything, none of it does." He pushed buds into his ears and spun through his Perse's menu, picking something to suit his mood.

"What are you listening to?"

He turned it down. "What?"

"What are you listening to?"

"Music."

"Can I listen?" She pointed at the Ent.

He replaced the buds and held the Perse out to her, she took it from him and put it on the input plate.

"Play current." She said.

The music started, she frowned.

"What's this?" She said.

"You don't like it?"

"It's, it's OK. You not got any Chanks?"

He went over and pulled it from the station. "Chanks!"

"I like Chanks."

"Yeah baby yeah baby you know you done me good."

She smiled and continued the song. "Yeah baby, yeah baby now I'm gonna do you better."

"Such lyrics."

"Trees in green dresses, what was that one about?"

"It doesn't matter."

"I've not heard it before."

"It's old, before you were born."

"You're not much older than me."

"No."

"Then why?"

"Why?"

"Why do you listen to it?"

"I like it." He stubbed out his cigarette. "It reminds me."

"Of?"

"What I lost."

"Always so cryptic."

He smiled. "The woman I." He paused, rubbed his face, thought of what he wanted Maya to know, what he was prepared to share with her.

"The woman I worked with, well she would say worked for, she didn't have much time for words. Guess I picked up her habits."

"And she listened to that?"

"God, no, she hated my music, said it was depressing. She liked pop."

"Sounds like she has taste."

"Taste!" He shook his head, lit a cigarette.

Maya toyed with the label on her bottle.

"Where is she?" She said.

"Who?"

"The woman." She arched an eyebrow. "You worked for."

"I don't want to talk about her."

"Fine, what do you want to talk about?"

"Nothing."

"OK, what do you want to do then?"

"Maya."

She pouted.

"You said you would teach me, you know, to defend myself."

"Right." He drained his bottle, dropped the cigarette in to it and stood up.

"Come here."

She walked to him, he lifted her arms posing her.

"This is a basic guard, your left is for jab and parry, you keep your right back as your stronger arm."

He kicked her feet apart.

"Stand like that, weight on the balls of your feet."

He stepped back and mirrored her stance.

"Throw a punch, left hand, aim for my face."

She jabbed and he batted it to the side, followed through with a right that stopped on her chin.

"That's a counter, you try."

She parried his left and punched him in the face with her right, he stumbled back.

"I guess I deserved that." He rubbed his chin, smiled, waved off the alarm in her eyes.

"Try again."

She repeated the move, he dodged the counter, responded with a left hook he touched to her side.

"Good, again."

As she grew confident he increased the pace, introduced

new punches, showed her how to counter them.

"Now kicks." He looked at her skirt. "It might be tricky to kick in that."

She undid the zip and let it fall to the floor.

"Don't you ever wear underwear?"

"There never seemed to be a point."

"Um. OK. Despite what you've seen on the Ent, kicks to the head and the upper body aren't that effective. They're showy and leave you vulnerable. They're best against the legs and groin. This is a front kick – straight through see? This is a side kick, go for the knee."

He demonstrated both of them.

"You try." He said, making sure to keep out of range.

"You will have to practise all these on a bag." He said.

"Where will I get one of those?"

"We'll sort one out later, but that's your basics."

That's it? It doesn't seem like a lot?"

"A real fight is brutal and fast, if it isn't over in a minute then you should have run away."

"You'd run?"

"I have done."

"What if they have hold of you?"

She stepped towards him and grabbed his arms. He broke the lock and swept her leg dropping her to the ground.

"Ow!"

"Sorry, a lot of it is muscle memory, you will just have to practise."

She got back to her feet.

"Show me that."

He guided her through the move, let her try it out. She laughed when she threw him to the floor, dropped on top to grind her groin against his.

"I like this better, don't you?"

She smiled and kissed him, he resisted, made to push her off then relaxed, probed her mouth with his tongue, felt hers pushing back. She undid his jeans, dragging them down and freeing his cock, sliding it into her she rocked back and forth, pulled her blouse over her head, he reached up to her breasts, she put her hands over his and leant back, speeding up her movements as he thrust into her.

"Oh yes, oh yes, do it to me daddy." She moaned.

He stopped, she opened her eyes and looked at him. "What is it?"

He pushed her off and walked into the bathroom.

"Chris?"

She sat on the floor not understanding what had just happened. He came back out, his trousers fastened up.

"Chris?"

He sat in one of the chairs, lit a cigarette.

"What was that daddy shit?" He said.

"I thought you would like it."

"It was, it was, wrong."

"I, I'm sorry." She didn't know what to say, she had never been with a man who hadn't paid for it, she just assumed that is what they all liked, that is what they all wanted.

"Forget it."

He took a beer from the minibar.

"Do you want to try again? I won't speak."

"Maya, I don't know what I want." He held out the cigarettes to her.

"Other than to kill Marshall?"

"Yes, other than that."

"OK." She lit her cigarette and stood up.

"Let's go kill him then."

Minus Five

Waking, Cam kept her eyes closed assessing the situation, remembering. A discrete five star hotel in the centre of Paris, the credit on her card pre-empted any awkward questions. Gracious smiles and of course madams (to her continuing annoyance) as they were shown to their suite. After a shower she collapsed in to the bed, ignoring John's pestering she had fallen into a deep sleep, able at last to relax.

She sat up, John grumbled and rolled away taking the duvet with him, she stared at his back, thinking about what she would do with him, what she should do, his desire to come with her, work with her, was foolish, the dreams of a boy who knew nothing of life and how hard hers could be. Understandable him wanting revenge but sometimes you just had to leave it, walk away. She played with the bandage on her stump, the doctor dressing the wound had expressed dismay that she hadn't kept the finger, the cut had been clean, a straight forward reattachment. '<I wasn't thinking clearly at the time.>' her response to their regret.

She padded across the thick carpet to the bathroom, used the toilet, splashed water on her face, dabbed it dry being careful to avoid her nose, checked her appearance in the mirror, eyes bloodshot, the flesh around bruised, but sunglasses and make up would hide that, as if it had never happened. Robes hung behind the door, she pulled one on and walked out to the balcony that looked out over the city, sat down on one of the chairs clustered around a small table and lit her first cigarette of the day. She scrolled through the room service menu, picking breakfast for the pair of them, leant back and closed her eyes, soaking in the warmth of the morning sun.

The door chimed, she stretched and stood, walked over to open it allowing the waiter to push the trolley in to the room, she tipped them with the card, closed the door behind them. She poured out a cup of coffee and took it and a croissant back to the balcony.

John woke, confused, not sure where he was, he sat up and rubbed his eyes looking around for Cam. He needed a piss and ran to the bathroom, coming out in a robe the match of hers.

"Morning." He said, his tone bright and cheerful.

She nodded back at him, exhaled a plume of smoke.

"Breakfast?" He said indicating the trolley. Uncertainty colouring his words, not sure as to his role in this relationship, what the rules were, the boundaries. She turned her palm up in a gesture that he took to be go ahead and so he fell upon the food, stacking up a plate, making a milky sweet coffee to go with it.

He sat beside her, began to construct a sandwich from the meat and cheese.

"Don't you love croissants?" He said.

"They're OK, I would have preferred pork and rice."

"For breakfast?"

"Yes, for breakfast."

"Sounds weird."

She smiled. "I always thought eating cereal with milk was weird."

"That's not weird."

"It is to me."

"Most people have cereal in the morning."

"In the West."

"Yes." He squinted. "Where're you from Cam?"

"It doesn't matter, it's where you're going that counts."

"Hmm." He was getting a bit tired of her gnomic utterances. "Can I have a cigarette?"

"You worked out how you're going to pay for them?"

"Uh? How about sex?" His smile sly.

"Wouldn't you have to be any good?"

He pouted. "I'll work for you."

"What can you do?"

"You'll have to train me."

"So I pay you and I have to teach you? Doesn't sound like a good deal to me."

He lit his cigarette and leant back.

"Think of it as an investment."

"An investment?"

"Yes, the boarding school, how much would that cost?"

"I don't know, not looked in to it, doubt more than quarter of a mill."

"Wow." He gulped. "Well instead of doing that you train me, if after you reckon you've spent two hundred and fifty thousand on me you think I'm not paying my way, then we part company."

"And you would pay me back?"

"You were going to spend the money anyway."

"Be worth the money to get rid of you."

"Oh, OK." A desperate look in his eyes. "Call it one fifty, and I will owe you it as well."

She dipped croissant in her coffee.

"Give me till the end of the day to think about it."

He smiled. "What shall we do till then?"

She laughed at his expression. "You not fucked out?"

"I reckon I could do it another time." He grinned. "Maybe a couple."

Paris, it wasn't what he imagined it to be, just another dirty city, he could be at home if not for the overheard conversations in French, or the occasional glimpse of the tower on the skyline flashing a thousand colours. The weather was better than home, the sun beating down from a clear sky, he was glad he had picked a T-shirt and shorts from the hotel shop, sandals completing the look, Cam had gone for similar with a pair of flip-flops not unlike the ones she had bought at the pawn shop. Their old clothes thrown in the trash, for John another piece of his old life gone, reluctant to let his shirt fall in to the bin until Cam took it from his hands with a tut. Fed up of his sullen mood she had suggested they go out and now they looked like all the other tourists enjoying a walk round the city. John's frustration increased at Cam's haphazard route.

"What are we doing?" He said.

"I'm showing you Paris." She lit a cigarette and waved her hands about.

"Oh, right, thanks."

"Not impressed?"

He shrugged. "I guess."

"There we go with the guessing again."

"What do you want me to say?"

"Nothing, unless you have something worth saying."

"Like what?"

She blew out smoke. "Not 'I guess'."

John resisted pulling a face, kept his tongue in his mouth rather than poking it out at her.

"Can I borrow some money?"

"What for?"

He pointed at the Perses in a shop window. "To get one."

"Why?"

"For, you know, well it's a Perse."

"I never saw the point in them."

"You've never had a Perse?"

"No."

How could she live without one? "What about all your stuff, contacts, music and photos, all that?"

"If I can't keep it in my head then I don't want to rely on it."

"Really?"

"You come to rely on things like that then you put yourself at risk."

"But photos, music, you can't keep those in your head."

"What if you lose it?"

"You can back it up."

"Where?"

"In the cloud."

"The cloud." She sucked through her teeth.

"At your house then."

"I don't have a house."

"Where do you live?"

"Where ever the work is."

"You don't have a home?"

"No."

"Wow."

"Nothing that I don't have in here." She tapped her temple.

"But then, what have you to show for your life?"

She stopped, what did she have? Just her memories, when she died that would be it, as if she never existed.

"I guess some will remember me." The ones whose lives she had destroyed. "It doesn't matter anyway."

"Then what's the point?"

"We have been through this John, there isn't any." By their bones this boy was annoying, his questions showed up her shortcomings, mocked her carefully manufactured ambivalence.

"Can I borrow some money then?"

She sighed. "Your tab is getting pretty big."

"I offered a way to pay it off." He grinned, it widening when she smiled back. She shook her head and entered the shop.

"This is the place."
She threw her stub into the street and pointed at a nondescript door, a small plaque announcing that M. Arnaud had offices there.

"<David, it's Cam.>" She smiled at the camera and listened for the buzz of the catch releasing, pushed it open and went in, forcing John to scurry in before it swung shut. She pushed the lift call button.

"Who are we seeing?"
"An associate of mine, someone who might have some work for me, or know of where I can get some."
"He's called David?"
"Yes."
"Then why does it say M. Arnaud on the door?"
"Monsieur."
"Oh."
"Yes." She ushered him into the lift and pressed the button for the fifth floor. It groaned and creaked as it ascended, John played with his new Perse, marvelling at the camera present on the European model. He focused it on her, pulled a face when she pushed him away, took a photo of the passing walls visible through the iron scroll-work instead. She watched him, amused by the pleasure he was getting from the thing but feeling no urge to get one herself, it could be compromised and the contacts scrutinised, used against you. Music didn't matter and photos were incriminating or reminded you of pain.

She tsked. Puzzled, he looked at her, she twisted her mouth, a slight shake of her head. The lift shuddered to a halt and she pulled open the door, he followed her out in to the corridor towards the office at the end. Cam entered without knocking, the room small and cluttered, dominated by a large desk. The man sat behind it, middle aged, slate grey eyes and blond hair, got up and walked round to her.

"<Cam! It's good to see you again!>" He said, embracing her and kissing both cheeks.

"<And you David, this is my associate John.>"

"<Hello John.>" He held out his hand.

"Um <Hello, how are you?>" John said, shaking it.

"<I'm good, and yourself?>"

"Um." Helpless John shrugged, unable to think of a reply.

"<He doesn't speak French.>" Cam said.

"<Ah, he's English, yes?>"

"<Yes.>"

"<And where did you find him?>"

"<England.>"

"<Of course!> Welcome John, we can speak English if you prefer?" His speech heavily accented and hard to understand.

"Thank you."

Cam tapped a cigarette from a pack. "You mind if I smoke?"

"Of course." He pointed at an ashtray on the desk, gestured to the two chairs in front of it.

"Thanks." She lit it, ignored the pestering look from John and sat down. David returned to his seat, leant forward, his elbows on the desk, and smiled at them.

"So how have you been Cam?" David noticed the bandage on her hand. "A few scrapes eh?"

"Rough with the smooth, same as it ever was."

"Certainement, ah certainly. You in Paris for long?"

"That depends, you got any jobs?"

"A couple, but I'm not sure if they would interest you, a bit below you, if you know what I mean."

"<A training mission could be what I'm looking for.>"

"<For your associate? He wants to get into the business?>"

John frowned, annoyed that they had reverted to French.

"<He's expressed an interest, but I don't know if he's up to it.>" Cam said.

"\<He's awfully young.\>"
"\<We were all young once.\>"
"\<True.\>"
"So, you might have something for me?"
"Let me think, ah yes, a collection, a man owes, another man wants his money back."
"Leg breaking!"
"I said it was beneath you."
She blew out smoke, thought then nodded. "They in Paris?"
"Yes, in the 3rd arrondissement."
"What do they owe?"
"Eight thousand."
"And my take?"
"Twenty percent."
She looked at John. "You ready to earn some money?"

Leg breaking, what did she mean? Getting someone to pay up, threatening them with violence, is this what she did? She tilted her head, waited for his reply.

"I guess so." He said, saw her scowl and said. "Yes, I'm ready."
"Good." She ground her cigarette out in the ashtray, said to David. "What's the address?"
"I'll… oh yes of course, you don't have a Perse. I have it here, do you want me to write it down?"
"Just tell me it" She said, ignoring John's smile.

Outside the building Cam looked for a cab. Thinking about the conversation John shoved his hands in to his pockets, stared at his feet.

"I'm to beat someone up?" He said.
"It may come to that, yes."
"To get them to pay?"
"They owe money, no one made them borrow it."
"But."
"You said you wanted to learn what I did."
"And that's what you do?"

"Not really, but you have to start somewhere and the principles the same."
"We going there now?"
"No time like the present."
"But what will I do?"
"Ask them for the money."
"And if they say no?"
"Make them say yes."

Make them say yes. John was silent in the cab, this was it, she had decided to train him, or this was a test, either way he had to succeed, to get money from this man, Henri Dumas, who owed it to Arnaud, or someone that Arnaud was a middleman for, he wasn't sure what the relationship was. Eight thousand Euros and they would get twenty percent, that would be, sixteen hundred, no wonder Cam had looked dismissive. She had just stolen ten million, a couple of grand was nothing to her, he realised she was testing him, seeing if he was worth taking on, worth training.

The cab pulled up outside Dumas's apartment.

"You ready?" She said.

His face pale, John nodded in reply and got out. He checked the numbers printed on the intercom set in to the wall by the entrance, Dumas was on the third floor. Now he had to get in, he pushed the door, locked. Cam watched him offering nothing.

In the Threads they would ring another bell, claim to be a delivery man or some such, get buzzed in that way. But he would need to speak French to do that, or he would have to ask Cam to do it for him. 'Failed at the first hurdle' he thought. The door opened and a man stepped out, glanced at them then walked away. John caught it before it closed, held it open for her.

"Lucky." Cam said, following him in.

Ten Minus Ten

Another ancient lift took them to the third floor, Cam walked to the window overlooking the street. She sat on the sill and pulled her feet up, leant back against a jamb and lit a cigarette. John approached the apartment door, raised his hand to knock, hesitated, rapped on the wood and waited.

The door swung open and John faced a man in his early thirties, rich looking, tanned skin, neatly trimmed beard, expensive clothes.

"<Yes?>" A voice laced with impatience.

"Um, Monsieur Dumas?"

"<Yes, what do you want?>"

"Um, I don't suppose you speak English do you?"

"Yes, a little, what is it that you want?"

"Ah, that's a relief, I wasn't sure how I was going to go about this."

"About what?"

"It's about the money you owe, eight thousand Euros, I have come to collect it."

"You?"

"Yes, me."

"Fuck off kid." The door was slammed in his face, at a loss John stood staring at it.

"That went well." Cam said. She dropped from the ledge and ground her cigarette out on the floor. She stepped out of her flip-flops and walked past him to bang on the door.

"Dumas?" She said when the man opened it.

"<Yes, who are you?>"

He looked over her shoulder at John.

"Ah, you brought your mother?"

She punched him hard in the solar plexus, winded he stumbled back into the flat. She followed him in and swung a kick at his knee dropping him to the floor.

"<I have come for the money, eight thousand.>"

"<I don't have it.>"

She kicked him in the stomach, causing him to curl around it.

"<The money.>"

"<Please, don't, I can get it.>"

"<Get it.>"

He struggled in to a sitting position, looked up at her from the floor.

"<It will take some time.>"

She kicked him in the face, knocking him backwards against the wall.

"<I don't have time.>"

"<Please, no more.>" He held his hands up. "<I can get you it, I need a few hours, this afternoon.>"

"<This afternoon it's ten grand.>"

"<OK, that's OK, ten thousand, this afternoon, I will have it.>"

"<Try anything clever and I will fuck you over, do you understand?>"

"<Yes, I understand.>"

"<I will be back this afternoon.>"

She walked out of the flat and put her shoes back on, pushed the button to call the lift. John looked at the curled up man on the carpet, snivelling, hands pressed to his face, wondered if he should go and punch him, show Dumas that he meant business too.

"John." Cam said, pulled open the lift door and stepped in. He hurried to join her, stood in silence beside her for the ride down. It clanked to a stop and they got out on the ground floor. She lit a cigarette, held the pack out to him.

"What now?" He said.

"We go back in the afternoon, you been to the Louvre?"

"No." He held the apartment block's door for her, she frowned at the gesture, walked through.

"Not worth bothering with, unless you like queueing, we'll

go to the Guimet." She stepped out into the road to hail a cab.

"<Two beers.>" Cam said to the bartender, pulled out a stool and sat down. John took the one next to her, picked up the bottle placed in front of him and nodded his thanks. He rotated it in his hands, staring at the unfamiliar label, sipped and grimaced at its taste. Cam tilted hers back, put it down half empty and lit a cigarette, left the pack on the bar between them. He reached for them, paused, hand drawn back.

"You're quiet." She said.

"I guess." He had failed, had to let her step in and get the money for him. She'd given him the twenty percent for 'his effort', kept the extra two grand for herself. It felt like that would be all, that she was giving him some money and, soon, a train ticket to a boarding school. He had failed and now it was over, if he wanted revenge it would be on his own, find the means without her.

"Guessing again." She finished her bottle, spun on her stool to look out at the room. So he had failed getting the money, it had been a big ask, more to see how he would react, she hadn't expected him to get it, not without her to back him up, it was how he dealt with it that interested her, and in that he had performed badly. She had been alone for a while now, the idea of having a partner appealed, especially someone young she could mould how she saw fit, bind them to her, make them loyal, not like Holt who had betrayed her when it mattered most. But was John the right one? Did he have the determination, the toughness for the life she led? Boarding school might be the best option for both of them, she should stick with hired hands and casual fucks when she felt the need. She blew smoke from her nose and closed her eyes, leant back against the bar.

"<You look like you are carrying the weight of the world.>"

"Huh?" She looked at the man standing in front of her. Tall, smooth shaven, dark hair brushed back disguising a thinning crown.

"<I said, the weight of the world, it's on your shoulders yes?>"

"<It sometimes feels that way.>"

"<And such lovely ones as well.>"

His brown eyes travelled from them to her breasts then to her face, he smiled.

"<My name is Patrice, may I get you another drink?>"

John noticed the interaction and twisted his stool round to them.

"What's he want?" He said.

"<Who is this boy?>" Patrice said.

"<He's mine.>"

"<You're his mother?>"

"<You know how to flatter a woman.>"

"<My apologies, I wouldn't have believed you to be old enough anyway.>"

"<Good recovery.>"

"<Can I get you a drink?>"

"<Brandy.>"

"<Excellent, something with a little age though hey? Something perhaps older than your friend.>"

"<And coke.>"

"<You're joking yes?>"

"<I rarely joke, I haven't got the timing.>"

John slid from his stool and stepped closer to her. "What's he want Cam?"

"He's chatting me up."

"And you're letting him?"

"Why not?"

"<He's English? Oh dear> Hey kid, why don't you leave the adults to talk?"

"Why don't you fuck off?"

"You need to learn some manners."

"Are you the one to teach me?"

Patrice stepped closer and jabbed his finger into John's chest. John pushed it to the side and threw a wild punch that failed to land putting him off balance, unprepared for the counter to his stomach and then the follow up to his chin that blurred the world leaving him dazed, not seeing the next one that floored him.

Patrice kicked him knocking the air from his lungs, he tried to grab the foot, failed to grasp it and watched it pull back for another strike that Cam blocked with her shin.

"<That's enough.>" She said.

"<He needs to be taught a lesson.>"

"<He's learnt it.>"

"<I'll decide that!>" Patrice raised his hand to slap her, she dodged the blow, picked up her beer bottle and hit him with it, crunching in to his cheek bone, bringing it back on the return swing to hit him again. Winded, trying to get his breath back, John watched her strike the man, surprised that the bottle didn't smash like in the Threads instead thumping against Patrice's flesh with each swing until he collapsed to the floor.

"<I said enough.>" She dropped the bottle and kicked him hard in the face, spilling loosened teeth.

John used the bar to get back to his feet, gripping its edge he tried to quell the shaking, get a hold on the fear and shame he felt for the second time that day.

Cam lit a cigarette, looked round the room.

"Time to leave." She said, dropped money on the counter and headed for the door. John caught up with her on the street, hung by her side unsure what to say.

Offering him the pack she said. "Do you know why you lost?"

He took one, accepted the lighter with a thin smile.

"He was better than me."

"That's why."
"Because he was better?"
"No, because you thought he was."
"I don't understand."
"If you go into a fight fearing that you might lose then you go easy on your opponent. You think that if you do lose then they will go easy on you. They might just slap you about a bit but you won't be hurt too bad. You accept that you might lose and so you do."
"And you don't think you're going to lose?"
"I don't fight unless it's to win."
"How do you know you're going to win?"
"You offer no quarter, no mercy, no consideration for the consequences."
"And then you win?"
"Then you make sure you win."
"Right."
She grabbed his arm, hustled him towards the hotel.
"Fighting makes me horny."

She rolled off him and sat up, reaching for the cigarettes on the side table.
"You changed your mind?" She said.
"About?" He said, still dozy from the sex he found it hard to think.
"This life, you still want it?"
"I thought you were going to ship me off to a boarding school, you know, after today."
"Yeah, you fucked up a lot." She lit a cigarette, tossed him the pack.
"Yes, I did."
She pointed the cigarette at him. "Good, no excuse."
"No." He rubbed his face and pushed up to lean against the headboard.

"You still think you're cut out for it?"
"Yes."
"It didn't seem that way."
"I just need to be taught how to fight."
"And other things." She winked.
He coloured. "I'm willing to learn."
"You seem a quick study."
His colour deepened and she laughed.
"If you want this life then you will need to toughen up."
He lit a cigarette, drew in the smoke.
"I'm ready."

"You need training and I don't have the time or patience for that. There's a group in Texas – the 'Sons of Righteous Liberty'."

"Righteous Liberty?"

"They're terrorists, though they would call themselves freedom fighters, they're trying to gain independence from Mexico. You can spend a few months with them"

"Go to Texas?"

"Well, Arizona actually, they have a training camp there. They owe me a favour as I brought down the government a few years back, turned it into the anarchy that welcomes their ilk."

"You brought down a government?"

"Yes, that's my speciality, you don't think I'm a bonebreaker do you?"

"Is that what you were doing back home?"

"Sort of, Marshall seemed like a small fry who had a lot of money, I underestimated him."

She rubbed at the bandage on her hand.

"How did you get caught?"

"Being too careful, you heard of Machiavelli?"

"No."

"Guy from Italy, said you shouldn't leave behind people who would seek revenge."

"You were going to kill him?"

"Yes, that was the idea."

"Oh." If she had just left with the money he would never have met her, his parents would still have been alive. Being too careful had cost him everything. He tried to keep it in check, not to cry in front of her, make him look weak, make her change her mind. He picked up the Perse from his bedside table and swiped through the screens.

"Niccolò Machiavelli – The Prince." He said.

"That's him."

"I'll read it."

"I'll think of a few others."

"Though you said you were too careful." He smiled at her.

"Yeah, it pays to think for yourself sometimes."

"Huh." He used the credit she had loaded on his Perse to buy it, started reading the introduction. She watched him, smoke curling from her lips, wondered if she was making a mistake.

"John?"

"Yeah?" He looked up from the screen.

"You serious? You want this life?"

"Yes." He was, wasn't he?

"They're religious types, you'll have to say you believe in Jebus."

"It's Jesus."

"Whatever, I have my own Gods to ignore."

Seven

Entering the Police Station, Nick Jenkins waved at the Duty Officer to get buzzed through the door in to the squad area. He stopped by a vending machine in the hallway and pressed the numbers for a white coffee, followed by a tea, held them by the thin plastic rim until he reached the main office where he had to transfer them to one hand while he messed with the reader that allowed him access. He grimaced, the heat permeating the thin plastic was beginning to burn his skin, making his swipes more frantic until he heard the beep and the buzz of the lock. He pushed the door with his shoulder and shuffled through, put the cups down on a convenient desk and rubbed his fingers in an effort to ease the pain.

"Molten lava." Harry Underwood looked up at him.

"What?" Nick said.

"Molten lava, I don't know how they get them so hot, out of a machine an all."

"Tastes like lava too."

"Not even that good."

Nick laughed. "Aye, but beggars can't."

Harry pulled a face, his expression dismissive. "Canteen's just down the corridor."

"Not spending that kind of cash."

"Not on her anyway." Harry jerked his head to where D.I. Charlotte Fuller sat.

"She's not so bad."

Harry sniffed. "Maybe not to look at, but under that tasty exterior is a steel ball crusher."

"Bet you'd like her to crush your balls Harry."

"Thirty four years of marriage, my balls ain't much to speak of."

Not wanting to talk, or even think, about Harry's old man scrotum, Nick picked the cups up by the rim, gave a nod and walked over to his desk in the corner facing his superior.

"Morning ma'am." He put the coffee down in front of her.

Charlotte looked up from her screen, glanced at the clock on the squad room wall and back to him.

"Good morning, thanks." She acknowledged the drink. "Nice of you to show up today."

Nick glanced at the time on his Perse.

"I'm here now." He said, refusing to apologise.

"Yes, at last. They got an ID on your pimp's killer."

"He wasn't my pimp."

"Touchy, I meant the case you've been asking about, Anthony Lennon, male, twenty-seven, numerous convictions for the promotion of prostitution. Surprisingly little jail time, jammy bugger seems to have always got away with it."

"Well until he was killed."

"There is that." She sipped her drink and grimaced. "How long have you been my D.S? Nearly two years? And you still forget the sugar!"

She rummaged in her desk drawer for a sachet and tore off its side, dumping the contents into the cup.

"Well I knew you had your own supply." He smiled. "So who was the perpetrator?"

"Prozzy, name of Maya Hughes, multiple priors, prostitution, possession, the usual."

She flicked her screen sending the charge sheet to his. He glanced at the details, no fixed address, known associates all criminals, the most frequent being Lennon.

"Wonder why she did it?" He said.

"Probably sick of him smacking her around, who cares?" She stirred her coffee with a stylus and sucked it dry.

"That's disgusting."

"Remember to put a bloody sugar in it next time then."

"You should give it up, that stuffs poison."

Charlotte curled her lip. "Better than some addictions."

He coloured, concentrated on typing a message to Marshall giving the girl's name and last location. Charlotte swiped her hand across her screen to lock it and stood up.

"The bank job yesterday, guard is conscious at last, we'll go and interview him at the hospital." She said.

"Why bother? Other witnesses said he was taken out first, doubtful he'll have anything useful to add."

"Procedure, Nick, procedure, we need to follow it no matter how pointless."

His Perse chirped the hook from the latest Chanks track, Charlotte rolled her eyes at him.

"Got a hot tip have you?" She said.

He glanced at the message 'FIND HER, BRING HER TO ME' and deleted it, dropped the Perse back in his pocket with a sigh.

"Boyfriend giving you grief?"

"You have no idea."

"You will have to put your love life on hold, we've got work to do."

Nick shrugged. "OK."

He needed to be out on the street anyway, find the girl for Marshall, fetch her like the good little dog he was.

Wide awake Maya lay in bed unsure what to do. She fidgeted, thinking about the shots of Grind in her bag, would she be able to sneak in to the bathroom without him noticing? She sat up and eased back the duvet, looked over to the other bed where he lay facing her, his eyes closed. She swung her legs round, feet touching the floor and stood.

"Where're you going?"

She started at his voice, blinked in surprise.

"The toilet." She said.

"OK." He stared at her, an expression of distrust, impatience on his face. She smiled at him, twisted her arms in a stretch that lifted the T-shirt she had been sleeping in up her thigh, watched him watching her, traced her tongue along her lip. He looked away, reached for his Perse on the bedside table, pushed buds in to his ears and closed his eyes. She dropped her arms and stomped off to the bathroom, slamming the door behind her. He flicked tracks, increased the volume, avoided thinking about the future by remembering the past.

Maya flushed and came back out into the bedroom, she looked at him propped half up on a pillow, chewed her bottom lip while she considered what to do. She could go back to bed, try and sleep, but knowing she had three shots of Grind, so close, so available, just made her want it, it was all she could think about. For years she had been forcibly woken from a drug induced stupor and pushed out onto the street to earn, or driven to a porn stop to act out punters fantasies on camera. Any free time she spent zoned out in front of the Ent in a Grind fuelled haze, giggling at the CellEnts and trash Threads whilst the drug dulled the pain and suppressed the fear, making everything OK.

She dressed in the clothes from the night before, occasional glances at him to see if he was watching her, frustration building when she realised he wasn't. She grabbed a pair of buds from the Ent stand and slumped in to a chair.

Lost in memories he let the music wash over him, reluctant to get up, to face the day, he had never been a good morning person and his partnership with Cam had only exacerbated it. Criminal activities seemed to go better at night. Or she just preferred it. She could sleep the day away, he had often found himself in the same position as Maya, bored and not knowing what to do. Killing time until it was time to go out and kill. Foolish thoughts, but it pointed to his answer. He should stop messing about and just do it, go to Marshall's house and end this.

"Have you seen the news?" Maya gripped him by the shoulder, shaking him until he opened his eyes.

"He's dead!" She pointed at the Ent.

"Who's dead?" He pushed her hand away, picked up his cigarettes and shook one free.

"That guy from the hotel - he was called Gareth Rockwell."

"Oh." He lit a cigarette, pushed his hair back from his face.

"Oh? That's it?"

He shrugged, blew out smoke. "What do you want me to say?"

"You killed him! We killed him." She started to shake, another man dead, another she was linked to.

He glanced at the article, recognised the man, his wife and children blurred besides him.

"Shame, but people die all the time."

"Not like that, the poor man, he didn't deserve to die."

"Who does?"

"Bad people, murderers, criminals."

"People like me?"

"Well, yes."

"I deserve to die?"

"Well, maybe more deserving than him."

"You don't know him, he could have been a right cunt."

"He seemed just ordinary."

"He was cheating on his wife for a start."

"That's not enough. Not to die, not in that way. Found bound in a room - what would his wife think?"

"He shouldn't have cheated on her then."

"He had kids!"

"Should've been at home with them then instead of out fucking whores."

"You are hopeless!" She grabbed her bag, slinging it over a shoulder and ran to the door. Wrenching it open she triggered the screamer, its wail pulsing through her, twisting her insides, dizzy she dropped to the floor with her hands over her ears trying to block the sound. He slammed the door and deactivated the unit, stood over her with a hand held out.

"Maya."

Curled up, she ignored him, tried to get her breath back, thick phlegm clogging her throat, she spat on to the carpet, wiped her mouth with the back of her hand. She got to her feet, leant against the door frame, tried to hold back the vomit, pushed him away and ran in to the bathroom.

"Maya?" He had followed her in, she stood with her hands gripping the sink edge, pale faced staring at her reflection in the mirror.

"That noise!"

"I warned you."

She splashed water on her face, used one of the thick fluffy towels to dry it.

"It will ease in a minute." He said.

"You didn't even flinch."

"You get used to it, trick is to experience it a few times."

Memories of the punishment box, dry Arizona heat, the wail of the screamer bouncing from the metal walls, laying in his own filth, tears streaming down his face, begging for it to end.

"I can't be part of this." She pushed past him, hesitant she approached the door, looked back at him.

"It's not on."

"I'm sorry Chris."

Silent he lit a cigarette, watched her leave, pushed the door shut behind her and reactivated the screamer.

"And that's all you remember?"

Nick closed the file on his Perse and rose from the chair beside the hospital bed.

"Thank you Mr Edwards." Charlotte said smiling at the man who lay in it. Her first words since introducing herself and Nick, she had remained standing by the door, allowing her subordinate to run the interview.

"If you recall anything else then please call either myself or D.S. Jenkins at the station." She said, leaving the room without waiting for her words to be acknowledged. Nick caught up with her outside, fell in to step beside her for the walk to the lifts at the end of the ward.

'Edward Edwards, what an idiotic name' Nick thought, the man hadn't seen anything. First thing he had known about the hold-up was a stream of bullets ripping through his flesh and shredding his organs. Fired for dereliction of duty in not preventing the robbery he would now have to rely on charity, hooked three times a week to a dialysis machine instead of kidneys, shitting into a bag instead of an intestine.

"Poor bugger." Charlotte said, echoing his thoughts.

"Should have done his job."

She stopped, her expression a mixture of surprise and disgust. "You can be a heartless arsehole at times."

"Shouldn't have taken the job if he wasn't prepared to take the risks."

"I'll remind you of that when we catch up with the robber."

"I'll be hiding behind you."

"As always." She started walking. "What did you get from that bookies fire?"

"You think they're connected?"

She stopped again. "No, do you?"

"No."

"Then why suggest it?"

"I don't know, why did you mention it?"

"Because you're supposed to be investigating it."

"Nothing to it, bloke drives his car into a betting shop."

"On purpose?"

"Probably an accident."

"Then why didn't he stop around?"

"Maybe he was drunk?"

"Who owned the car?"

He consulted his Perse. "Gareth Rockwell."

"Why is that name familiar?"

"Old boyfriend?"

"Funny, you done a search?"

"Of course." He tapped the screen, kicking one off.

She pressed the call button for the lift.

"Oh shit." He said.

"What?"

"He's dead, found him in a hotel room, choked to death on his sock."

"I thought I had heard that name, was on the news this morning. Was that after he rammed the bookies?"

"Tee oh dee makes it unlikely."

"So someone ties him up and steals his car then drives it into a betting shop."

"Looks like it."

"Do we think that's suspicious?"

"There's no need to be sarcastic."

"What's the name of the hotel? We'll call in on the way back to the station."

Minus Four

Shielded from the heat of the midday sun, John sat smoking on the verandah staring out at the waves. He looked back through the open doorway at the bed in the one room beach shack they had been renting on Koh Tansay for the past two months. One in the afternoon and Cam still slept, she could sleep all day, and often did, it made him restless, frustrated. Already he had run along the beach before taking a swim followed by a late breakfast at a local café; one of the few places that had electricity, giving him chance to charge his Perse for a fee.

For six years they had been on the move, never stopping longer than a job required, short breaks in between but nothing like this, in the main it was time spent looking for the next opportunity. He had lived well, better than he had ever imagined, Cam didn't believe in saving money, she took her pleasures when she desired them, no expense spared. Which made this stay in the hut even more puzzling. Two months with nothing lined up, living frugally, lazy days on the beach and slow nights in the bars. At first he had enjoyed the time with her, the absence of pressure, the lack of danger, the fear of dying no longer foremost in his mind. But now he was beginning to miss it, the adrenaline of a shoot out, the satisfaction of a job well done. If she wanted to stay here then maybe he should take advantage of the time off, go back to England and kill Marshall. He had the skills, the means and the money, what was stopping him?

He should tell her he was going, that it was time for him to keep his promise.

John rocked the chair back onto four legs and stood. He went through the door to the small kitchen area, just a propane hob and a tap to a water tank filled twice a week by a bowser brought down the beach by donkey. He lit the stove and put on a pan to boil, placed a cracked plastic filter on top of a cup and shook in a good handful of the local dark roasted coffee grounds.

The rest of the room was sparsely furnished, an old battered table pushed against one wall, a large bed they had moved to the centre of the room to be under a rope operated fan, that he, always he, would tug on to move the heat around when the air became stiflingly oppressive. Cam lay on it, a single sheet covering her, her eyes closed, one arm under the pillow. He leant over and whispered her name. She smiled and opened her eyes.

"Where's my fucking coffee?"

"It's coming." He lit two cigarettes and handed one to her, taking it she sat up.

"How's it healing?" She nodded at his tattoo, he touched it, traced the line from his heart curling round his torso.

"Seems fine, could be a shopping list."

"It says John McPhereson, born in England, travelled the world ..."

"Killing and stealing?"

"Pretty much."

"Bit of a damning thing to have on your body, to have your confession I mean."

"It's more oblique than that, nothing too specific."

She touched her own, ran a finger down it to the new section that curled round her knee, done at the same time he had got his.

"Why Khmer?" He said.

She shook her head, drew on the cigarette and looked at him. "You haven't put it together have you?"

"Put what together?"

"You never asked me why I'm called Cam."

"I have, you never gave an answer."

"Cam isn't my given name."

"I guessed that."

"It's a nickname, got it when I started out, first few jobs were with a mercenary crew I hooked up with. They called each other after the countries they'd been born in, Utah, Missouri, one they called Frank cos he was from France."

"Frank from France?"

"Yeah, they were better at fighting than coming up with witty names."

She smiled. "Better at fucking too."

John blushed, stood up and walked back to the stove. He took the pan off, letting the boil subside before pouring it into the filter.

She watched him, her smile becoming wry, shook her head again. She tapped ash on to the rough wooden floorboards where it drifted in to the gaps.

"So they called me Cam." She said.

"From… from Cambodia?"

"Yes, from Cambodia."

Her smile broadened, and despite her chiding it still made him happy, reminded him of when they first met, the times in between, the things they had done together, marked in ink on his chest.

"Why are you telling me this?"

"To explain."

"Explain?"

"That this is where I am from, that this is my home."

"Koh Tonsay?"

She tsked. "Cambodia."

"Right."

"A place on the mainland, bit of a shithole, couldn't wait to get out. But here." She gestured at the beach visible through the window.

"I always liked the sea."

"OK." He took the filter off the cup and brought it over to her. "So why are you telling me this now?"

She sipped her coffee, placed it down on a small table at the side of the bed. She rubbed at the stump on her left hand, thought about her promise that she would never go back, and then looked at John. Eight years ago he had been a child with no idea of how his life would turn out, she had taken any hope for peace from him, caused his parents to be murdered, trained him to steal and kill, turned him into a male version of herself, she owed him for that, enough to break her vow.

"I think it's time for you to go home too."

"What?"

"The reason you started all this, stayed with me, rather than going to a boarding school, was to be trained so you could kill Marshall, get your revenge."

"You said revenge was for fools."

"And you're not a fool?"

"Cam."

She tapped ash, stared at the glowing tip rather than him.

"This is it for me, I'm getting tired, I've enough money and I've realised after all these years that this is all I really want."

"A beach hut?"

"Yes."

"You're quitting?"

"Yes."

"And what about me?"

She shook her head again. "That's my point John, it's time for you to go solo. I'll help you kill Marshall but then I'm done.

One last job."

"Kill him my way?"

"Your way?"

"I want him to suffer, take him down piece by piece, destroy his world, take his life when he has nothing left to lose."

"Too risky, if you're going to do it, then do it, kill him, job done, move on."

He frowned, anger on his face. "That would be too quick."

"Instant gratification is what I'm all about."

She ground her cigarette in the ashtray, hooked her hand in to his belt and pulled him to her, kissing him deep and hard, making his heart speed as she unbuckled his pants.

Eight

Charlotte pulled up outside the hotel and clicked on the hazards.

"Looks your typical dump." She said, peering out the windscreen at the entrance.

"Don't think their usual customers are bothered by décor." Nick said, checked his wing mirror and opened the passenger door. Charlotte got out her side, waiting for Nick to walk round the back of the car to join her.

"How'd you want to play this?" He said.

"We'll see what the receptionist saw, take it from there."

Inside the foyer Charlotte thumbed her Perse to bring up her warrant card and showed it to the receptionist.

"We're here about the body you found." She said.

"Oh yeah, some kinky shit that."

"You think it was a sex game gone wrong?" She leant forward, then pulled back as the stench of unwashed flesh struck her, a shirt clean on four days before stuck to the man's body, stained with food and sweat.

"I don't know what it was, I don't get paid enough to think." He sniffed, slicked back the little hair he had left and gave her a sullen look.

"Happen a lot then? People dying here?"

"Sometimes, I don't know, look I told the coppers that came here before all I knew, he was a just an ordinary punter, wanted a couple of hours, nothing else."

Charlotte stared at him, her eyes narrowed in thought. She nodded, swiped through her Perse and brought up Maya's photo.

"How about this girl?"

"Yeah, I remember her, John she was with booked five hours."

"Five hours?"

"Yeah, wondered what he had in mind." A leery grin giving her an indication of what he imagined.

"This was the same time as Rockwell checked in?"

"No, they were just leaving as he came in. I think they stopped and chatted to him. He came in and asked for a room, I didn't see what they did then."

"The man she was with, what did he look like?"

"The usual, maybe a bit younger, blond hair."

"Anything else?"

A shrug. "The number I get through here."

"OK, that will do for now."

"For now?" Alarm in his eyes.

"Yes, for now. We'll be in touch."

She turned, heading for the exit, Nick dropping in to step alongside her. Outside the morning had brightened, the sun a fitful presence from behind shredding clouds.

Unlocking the car Charlotte said. "So it seems your whore was here after she killed your pimp."

"She wasn't my whore, wasn't my pimp either."

He glared at her over the vehicle's roof, she ignored the look and got in the driver's side. Nick sat in the passenger seat and pulled the belt across his chest.

"Strange behaviour." She said.

"What is?"

"She kills him then goes back to turning tricks."

"Yeah, strange." Not paying attention he tapped a message on his Perse, put it back in his pocket.

"And here where Rockwell is murdered."

Nick frowned. "He wasn't stabbed though."

"What?"

"If that's what you're thinking, that she's started killing people, first her pimp and now a punter. Rockwell wasn't stabbed, he was tied up, left to choke to death."

"Still murder."

"Takes strength to subdue someone like that."

"Maybe she had an accomplice, the man who booked a room for five hours. That doesn't sound like someone who just wanted sex. Boyfriend maybe, maybe someone tired of sharing her, wanted exclusivity."

"Why Rockwell then?"

"They needed a car."

"What for?"

"To get away?"

"And instead they drove it in to a bookies?"

"Maybe they lost control?"

"Lot of maybes."

"Well what do you think? The car was taken from here, Rockwell was tied up, left to choke to death."

"OK, but it doesn't mean it was her. Witnesses said it was a man who got out of the car."

"One with blond hair."

"Yes, OK." He shrugged. "Too much of a coincidence."

"We'll check out her patch."

"What's the point in that? She wouldn't have gone back there."

"Good place to start, we can ask some of the other girls, see if they have an idea where she might go."

"As if they'd tell us."

This was getting worse, it looked now like Maya was involved in two killings, it would make it harder for him to deliver her to Marshall. He could see that Fuller was intrigued, she was like a dog with a bone when she got her teeth into something. One of the reasons she was a D.I. five years ahead of the curve, seven on him.

"You got somewhere to be?"

"Huh?" Nick said.

"You're acting like you've got something else you need to do."

"No, just don't see what the point is, she's small fry."

"She's linked to two murders."

"She only spoke to Rockwell."

"You got a better idea?"

"No." He sighed. "OK, let's go check her old haunts."

"That's more like it. Who knows, we might get a break."

She started the engine and pulled out to join the traffic heading across town.

Approaching St Augustus, Maya rang the bell and stood, made her way to the door as the bus pulled to a stop. She hitched the bag on to her back, her fingers touching the outer pocket feeling the comforting lump of Grind. She had three shots and the cash Chris had given her after he had murdered Lennon. She should have taken more money, the screamer had scrambled her mind, all thoughts gone except the desire to flee, to get away from that noise. She had run out of there without thinking, and over what? Because a man had died? Chris was right, who was he to her anyway?

Now she was alone and on the street, if Marshall found her, well she would be best to find him first, give her side of the story, explain that it wasn't her fault. Tell him where Chris was, take her beating and then what?

Back to whoring, nothing changed.

She could go back to the hotel, apologise to Chris, try and make it right with him. He had offered to train her, take her with him, a life of killing and stealing. Is that what she wanted? Normal people didn't kill for the sake of convenience, what sort of man was he to view others with such contempt? Is that what he would turn her into, was that really better than selling her body? At least she didn't hurt anyone.

Except herself.

But then she wasn't worth anything was she? Her mother had beaten that into her, a waste of space, a drain and a hindrance.

A mistake.

She chewed at her lip, trying to think it through, unable to see a way out her thoughts drifted back to the Grind, perhaps she should do a shot, find somewhere to hide out for a few hours sunk in oblivion.

Nick scrolled through the latest reports on his Perse.

"The bank robbery, ballistics reports confirmed the bullets were from 'Sharpe's Gun Emporium' on St. Verity. Uniforms are on their way to question the owner."

"Allowing civilian's firearms." She shook her head at the stupidity. "They should never have changed the law."

"It's not the guns that do the killing."

Charlotte glanced at him, unsure if he was winding her up. "What?"

"You have a right to defend yourself."

"Defend yourself? That's what we're here for." She touched the weapon on her hip.

"Might be too late, not right that it's only the criminals who have guns."

"No one should have a gun."

"Except us."

"Not even us, we've gone too far."

"At least he would've had to use I.D. to buy them."

"Doubtful it wouldn't be fake."

She tapped the wheel. "His description, could match the

man with Maya."

"That he was young? Anyway, witnesses said he had brown hair, that one was blond."

"Heard of hair dye?"

"Be a bit neat, same perpetrator for three major crimes, wrap it all up in one go."

"Three?"

"Bank job, Rockwell, bookies."

"And the pimp."

"What? You don't think Maya killed Lennon?"

"The question is more why would she kill him? I don't see how it's improved her situation."

"Maybe she got tired of being screwed."

"So she slit her pimp's throat?"

"That's what the evidence says."

"What if this man is her boyfriend? Maybe he got tired of sharing her."

"Seems too much of a coincidence."

"It all fits."

"If you force it."

"It feels right."

"Feels!" He snorted. "Women's intuition?"

She pressed her lips together refusing to answer him, concentrated on the road instead. They drove on to the seedier part of town.

"We could call in at the shop." Nick said, hoping he could distract her long enough for someone to grab the girl before they found her.

"Later."

Nick checked his Perse, spotted a tip alert, gave a sideways glance at Charlotte to check she wasn't looking and put a bet on.

"Well, well, well." Charlotte said, slowing the car.

"What's up?"

"Looks like we just passed your whore." She pulled over and stopped.

"She's not my whore." He craned his head round the seat to look out the rear window. It could be Maya, it was too far to make out the girl's face. If he had been on his own then he could have picked her up, delivered her to Marshall. But now? Fuller would want to take her in.

"Get out, I'll turn around and drive past. You approach her from this side, I'll cut her off if she runs."

"You sure it's her?"

"Get out. If it isn't then no harm done."

He scowled.

"Go on, before she moves on."

"Waste of time." He got out, slamming the door, crossed over the road and stopped to stare at the girl. She matched Maya's description, but where was the man? He looked around, nervous at the thought of a ruthless killer being somewhere nearby. He started walking, wondering if he should try and scare her, get her to run before Charlotte was in position, he could let Marshall know where she was then, let him do his own dirty work and pick her up. He fumbled his Perse from his pocket and started typing a message.

"Maya is it?"

He heard Charlotte say, looked up to see her grip the girl's arm.

"We have some questions for you."

He checked the room was clean, deactivated the screamer and shoved it in to the top of his bag. He needed to move the plan forward, take out Marshall, be done with all this messing around. He would check out the house, if Marshall was there then he would kill him, as fast as Cam had wanted him to, be done with it and then leave. Be out of the county by nightfall and the country by the morning. He pulled the door shut behind him and headed for the stairs at the end of the hall, down them and out of the lobby in to the street.

Outside he flagged down a taxi and told the driver to take him to Elysium Delights. He ignored the cabbie's comments and stared out of the window, mixed up in memories and plans, trying to get something formulated, to stop just drifting along. He had become unstuck since he lost Cam, didn't know what to do without her. Wondered what the point of it all was if he had nothing to show for his life, no one to share it with. Was that why he had allowed Maya to come with him, that she would fill Cam's place, or give some meaning to his existence? A sixteen year old prostitute! And to fixate on the first woman that he met, that showed an interest in him, however contrived, what did that say about him? He didn't have much experience with women, for someone who had spent years travelling the world he knew little about them and less about relationships. It had been Cam from the start. Well, there had been that girl, Purity, in the camp. But that had been nothing, or almost nothing, more clinging to another human to cope with the ordeal, to ease the pain, provide comfort. Two women, and now three if you counted the abortive fuck. Sex had meaning for him, he'd never had a casual relationship; a one night stand. Perhaps that was it, he should go to a bar and pick up a woman, or maybe pay for it, remove the romance from the act, stop him pining like a school boy for a whore.

The taxi pulled to a stop, the driver's words breaking into his thoughts.

"You want to go in guv? I'll need an address to give at the barrier."

He looked out of the window, his plan had backfired, he could see that now. There were two guards on duty, wearing large coats hiding something bulky. Taking out Marshall's businesses had alerted him to the threat, made him cautious.

"I've changed my mind, take me back."

"To the hotel?"

"Yeah, to there."

"It's your money guv."

He would go back to the hotel, wait there a day to give Maya a chance to come back. If she did then he would honour his promise, take her with him. Or maybe he should just leave it, be done with this place, get out now and put it behind him. Forget about revenge, forget about it all, rent a hut on the beach and let the world pass by.

Maya sat in the interview room, rubbing at her wrists where the ties had been cut off. The three shots of Grind in a see through bag labelled 'evidence' on the table in front of her. Opposite sat Fuller, the door opened and in came Jenkins juggling three cups of tea.

"D.S Jenkins has entered the room." Charlotte said.

"Here you go Maya, nice cup of tea." Nick said, placing them on the table and pushing a styrofoam cup towards her.

Charlotte took one of the others, grimaced at the lack of sugar and put it back down. She flipped through her Perse, bringing up the charge sheet.

"So Maya, possession of a controlled substance, doesn't look good."

"No." She shrugged, ignoring the tea and leaning back on her chair. "What happens now?"

"Ordinarily you would be fast tracked, a fine and a note on your record, perhaps even a custodial sentence if you got the judge in the wrong mood."

"OK." That didn't seem so bad, it would get her off the street, away from Marshall, at least for a little while.

"Ordinarily that would be it, you'd be back out whoring in no time. But there's the little matter of you murdering your pimp."

Maya's face drained of blood, she slumped forward.

"What?"

"Anthony Lennon." Charlotte scrolled down her notes. "Slit his throat, nasty."

"I didn't kill him!"

"They found your saliva on his face." Charlotte shook her head. "Very amateurish, almost too easy to solve."

"But, I didn't."

"Open and shut wouldn't you say D.S Jenkins?"

"I would." Nick looked pained, his thoughts on how he would explain this to Marshall.

"Provoke you did he? You look like you've a bit of a bruise there." She pointed at Maya's cheek. "Couldn't take it any more. You just lashed out?"

"I didn't."

"Plead to manslaughter, you'll be out in eight, five with good behaviour."

"Five years?"

"Yes, hardly any time at all. What are you?" She consulted her Perse, "Sixteen? Out by twenty one."

"I didn't."

"If you opt for not guilty then we will push for murder, that's thirty years with a minimum term of eighteen. You'd be nearing forty Maya, life almost over."

"I didn't."

Charlotte slammed her hand on the table causing the cups to jump, sloshing tea. "Stop saying you didn't Maya, we know you did. You spat on him! You slit his throat and then spat on him as he lay bleeding out. Think how that will play with a jury."

Maya held out her arms, palms up, pleading.

"I, I spat on him, but I didn't kill him."

"Then who did?"

"I don't know."

"Don't lie to me Maya, either you give me their name or we

charge you with murder."

"He said it was Chris."

"Chris what?"

"I don't know, I never asked."

"That's not enough, we need his full name."

"I don't know it. Please."

"This the man you were with at the motel?"

"Motel?"

"Yes, the place you murdered Gareth Rockwell."

"Wait, I didn't, I mean, Chris, he tied him up, I don't think he meant to kill him."

"He choked to death on his own sock, can you imagine that Maya?"

"I didn't want anything to happen to him, I said to Chris, I asked him not to. But."

"He had children Maya, they wont get to see their daddy again."

Maya rubbed her face, stared at the floor.

"I never met my father." Her voice soft, thinking of the things her mother had said about him, most of them mean. But, sometimes, there would be a wistfulness about what might have been, if he hadn't been killed crossing the road, too busy grinning like an idiot at her scan.

"Then you know how they feel, give them some sense of justice, tell me about this man Chris."

"I don't know much."

"Then I'm charging you with murder."

"Wait! I can tell you where he is."

Charlotte gave a thin smile.

"That will be a start."

Minus Three

"Wake up, we're here."

Cam pulled over to the side of the road and nudged John in the ribs. He grunted and sat up rubbing his eyes.

"I must have dropped off." He said, covered his yawn with a hand and looked out of the window, wondering if he would recognise anything, if it had changed as much as he had.

"Snoring like a pig." She said.

"I don't snore!"

"No, you don't." She conceded.

"You do though."

He grinned at her glare, picked the cigarette pack off the dash and shook a couple out, she accepted one from him, lit it and passed him the lighter. She waved her hand at the street they were parked on, nondescript, unremarkable, like a thousand others he had seen in the past eight years.

"Glad to be home?" She said.

He shrugged, blew smoke from his nostrils, tapped ash out of his open window.

"Glad? There's nothing for me here any more, all my family are dead." His voice catching on the last word. "Doesn't feel like home anyway."

Cam rubbed at the stump on her hand.

"I didn't think I would come back here."

He nodded. "It won't be for long."

"Be a fuck sight shorter if we went with my plan."

"He has to suffer Cam, or else what's it for?"

"For him being dead?"

"He'll be dead soon enough."

"Or us."

"We won't, he's a small town crook."

"I made that mistake before." She said, her missing pinky twinging with phantom pain.

"You didn't have me then."

She laughed. "Yeah, that was it. The missing ingredient."

"Month, two months tops and then on to the next job."

"For you, for me it's back to Cambodia."

"Home."

"Yes, home."

She started the car and pulled out into traffic.

"Remember leaving here?" John flicked his cigarette out of the window, turned to look at her.

"Leaving here?"

"All those years ago, when we met."

"What was that, five years?"

"Eight."

"Eight? Really? Well, well."

He shook his head, she lived in the moment, not caring what year it was, or even the day. Eight years, and the sight of her still made him catch his breath despite the streaks of grey in her hair and the lines around her eyes. She felt him looking and pursed her lips. "What?"

"Nothing."

She smiled and said. "Pass me a fucking cigarette."

Driving through the streets John looked for anything he could recognise, to fit himself into them as he had been before, eight years ago. He tapped a cigarette free, played with it, rolling it from finger to finger, flicked it up to his mouth, missed.

Cam laughed.

"You worked out a plan?" She said.

He leant down to pick the cigarette from the footwell, lit it before replying.

"Marshall said he owned the cops."

"Yes?"

"Then we start there."

"What do you mean?"

"We give them something else to worry about, I think we should kill the mayor."

"Kill the mayor? What the fuck are you thinking?"

"He must know what Marshall is up to, must be allowing it, he's as guilty, time he was taken out."

"This is your plan?"

"You don't like it?"

"It's fucking mental, it's not a plan."

"We've killed presidents, ministers, royalty, what's a mayor?"

She tapped the wheel with her fingers.

"Yes, I don't object to you killing them, I just don't see the point of it."

"The police will be mobilised looking for the killer, they won't have time to help Marshall. Once that's under way we'll take out his businesses, one by one, then him."

"Don't you think they will be looking for us?"

"We've been hunted before."

She tutted, ground her cigarette out in the ashtray.

"Isn't much of a plan."

"It's spontaneous, I thought that's what you were all about?"

"Fair point." She had been using Holt's playbook for the last ten years, adapting but not improving it. John was too much like her, she needed someone who had a different temperament, who liked to plan, to think of the consequences and prepare for them. One of the reasons she was calling it a day, she had run out of tactics, her ideas were becoming old, tired, easy to anticipate, negate. The last job had almost been a disaster, only saved by an excessive amount of violence.

A regrettable amount.

She was getting soft, she knew it, recognised the signs. Quick way to becoming dead.

"OK." She said. "We kill the mayor."

"Be easy, not much security in a place like this, walk up and pop him. Or maybe a car bomb would be better, add an element of mystery."

"Mystery!"

"Uncertainty then, be unexpected."

"A provincial town mayor being killed by a car bomb would be unexpected. They might call in the national terror squad."

"I think it's called anti-terror."

"That depends on your perspective."

She pulled over in front of a row of shops.

"Why we stopping?"

"If we're going to kill the mayor then we'll need more than what we have in the trunk."

He looked at the sign on the closest store.

"'Sharpe's Gun Emporium', what sort of name is that?"

"We need guns and he sells them, what's more to know?"

She got out of the car and headed to it. John followed her in, catching the door as it swung back jangling the bell. They walked to the counter behind which the proprietor sat cleaning a weapon. A middle aged man, hair thinning around a cup sized bald spot on the crown, face slack and lined, heavy wrinkles around his eyes from constant squinting. He had raised his head and was watching them approach, the unwelcoming look on his face replaced by a forced smile.

"Can I help you?" He said, trying to put some warmth in to his voice.

"We want to buy some guns." Cam said. "And related items."

"Of course. What can I get you?" He dropped a cloth over the gun parts and stood, spreading his arms out to indicate his inventory.

She pointed behind him. "That machine pistol, how much?"

"Ah, an excellent choice." He pulled a key chain from his pocket and unlocked the cabinet. "The Falcon nine fifty, as the name suggests uses fifty round magazines of nine millimetre parabellum." He handed it to her, she cycled the chamber, listening.

"Open bolt?"

"Of course."

"Cost?"

"Seventeen thirty plus VAT."

"What the fuck is VAT?"

The man coloured. "Value Added Tax, four point eight percent."

"Four point eight? Why the fuck not say five?"

"I do not control the county's tax policies madam."

Cam scowled, flashed a look at John who hid his smile.

"OK, the automatic, that a Penyama?"

"Indeed it is, madam knows her weaponry."

"Less of the fucking madam if you want to make a sale today."

"Of course." He handed her the gun, she sighted it on him, causing him to flinch despite knowing it was unloaded.

"They are six ninety each." He said.

"Plus VAT?"

"Of course."

"We'll take four machine pistols and two automatics, plus ammunition."

"How many rounds?"

"Two boxes per should do it."

She ran her hand along a rack of vests. "These ablative?"

"Yes, resistant for up to fifteen minutes of small arms fire. Twelve hundred each"

"Two of those as well."

"That is quite a list. You must be serious about home defence?"

"You can do it?"

"Of course, that comes to twelve thousand, five hundred and eighty four pounds."

"Fine. Wrap them up."

He smiled at her. "Excellent." His smile faded. "However there is a twenty four hour wait on all guns, and you will need a valid ID to purchase them."

Cam frowned. "Twenty four hours?"

"I am afraid that is the law."

"OK." She held out her card.

"Thank you." He scanned it and passed it back. "That is all in order Ms. Malone. They will be ready for you at eleven am tomorrow."

"Tomorrow then."

"Yes, tomorrow."

He watched them leave, waiting for the door to shut before he pulled out his Perse and scrolled through the numbers. Finding the one he wanted, he pressed dial and held it to his ear.

"Mr Marshall? Trevor Sharpe here.

Yes, the gun shop as you call it.

You told me to inform you if someone made an unusual order.

Yes, quite substantial.

No, they're coming back tomorrow at eleven am to pick them up.

Two, a man and a woman. Could be mother and son. She's quite striking, green eyes, black hair, foul mouth.

Him? Blond, brown eyed, average, run of the mill.

OK, I thought you would want to know.

Thank you Mr Marshall. Goodbye."

He disconnected and put the Perse down, pulled the cloth from the weapon and picked up one of the pieces to clean.

"Callan, it's Marshall."

"Mr Marshall sir."

Mike Callan pushed the girl off his lap and stood up, ignoring her indignant squeals he stepped past her heading for one of the private booths at the back of the strip club. He gestured at Roger Benks and Nigel Stoker, pointed at his Perse then up, signifying he had the boss on. He pulled the curtain closed behind him and sat down on the padded bench that ran along one side of the small room.

"You in the club?"

"Yes, Mr Marshall, keeping an eye on your business."

"More like fucking on my time."

"No, Mr Marshall, it's not like..."

"Save it. You know that gun shop on Saint Verity, run by some wanker who thinks he's from the eighteenth century or something?"

Callan squinted, thinking. "The Gun Emporium?"

"That's it. He's got a couple coming in tomorrow at eleven in the morning, I want you to pick them up, a man and a woman. I want you to go in heavy you understand?"

"For two people?"

"You lose them, you answer to me, is that clear?"

"Yes, crystal, Mr Marshall, sir."

"Good." He disconnected.

The curtain pulled back and Benks entered the booth followed by Stoker.

Callan put his Perse away and shifted along the bench to give them room.

"What was that about?" Benks said.

"Gun shop on Verity, Marshall wants us to snatch a couple from there."

"Easy enough."

"Get Henley, we need a van."

"For two people?"

"He said go in heavy, they must have a rep."

Benks shrugged. "He pays the bills."

"And takes his price if you fail." Stoker said, a twisted grin on his face.

"Doesn't he just." Callan said, thinking of Marshall's cellar and that chair. "Get the van, we meet here at ten tomorrow."

"Straight snatch?"

"You and Henley in the van, cut them off before they get in the shop. Me and Benks come up behind, bundle them in."

"Weapons?"

"Marshall wants them alive, beanbag rounds and tasers."

"Unless they prove difficult."

"You're quite the pessimist Stokes."

"Plan for the worst, don't get dead as that bloke said."

"Not sure it goes like that."

"Close enough."

"OK, SMG's for backup, but if we deliver Marshall two bloody corpses then you can do the explaining."

Nine

He sat at the table in his room, his weapons laid out on its surface. He picked up the knife, ran the blade across a whetstone and tested its edge on his thumb. Satisfied he returned it to the sheath on his belt and moved on to the guns. Broke each down in turn, clean, oil, reassemble, load, on to the next, the ingrained process automatic, familiar, calming. Once done, he topped up the magazines, pushing cartridges in against the spring, the action taking him back to the long hours spent in the camp, a bucket of ammo and a stack of clips. Purity making jokes, teasing him for his accent, brushing the hair from her face, deep brown eyes focused on his, a lingering touch on his arm. Sneaking from their tents after lights out to meet at the perimeter, laid side by side staring at the stars, fingers interlaced, feelings unspoken, a kiss.

Cam had come for him without warning, a job she needed him for cut his training short, no chance to say goodbye, his last view of Purity was through the fence, a hand half raised, in farewell or entreaty he wasn't sure, an arched comment from Cam he chose to ignore.

Idaho three years later, ambushed, trapped in a diner, fighting their way out to the alley at the back he had stopped, stunned to see her guarding the exit to the street. Her smile of recognition turning to confusion then pain, Cam shouting at him to wake up, reloading her pistol and firing again.

A knock at the door shook him into the present, he turned

the music down and went to check the screen. A woman, early thirties, the photo on her hotel badge hidden by her suit lapel. He tapped the flashing talk icon.

"What is it?" He said.

"Mr Redentor may I come in?"

"What do you want?"

"The guests downstairs have reported a leak, I need to come in and check your bathroom."

A leak? It felt wrong. He stared at her image wondering why they hadn't sent a plumber. Standing close to the camera she blocked his view of the corridor.

"Please Sir, it'll only take a couple of minutes."

"Come back later." He said.

"It is a matter of some urgency."

The screen showed the frustration on the woman's face, and something else that made his neck itch, a feeling that all was not quite right.

"I'm naked, come back in an hour." He said.

He clicked off the screen and began shoving his stuff into the bag, ignoring the knocking he put on his jacket, hung the machine pistols around his neck on their rope.

Chambered a round in each.

The door boomed, a shotgun breaker charge blowing it inwards, the screamer's howling disorientating the S.W.A.T. team attempting to enter, its subsonics bypassing their ear protection making them hesitant, confused, falling in to each other and blocking the entrance. He raised his left machine pistol and emptied it in a single burst, the rounds punching his assailants back in to the corridor. He kicked the door shut, let the empty gun drop to hang from the rope and lifted the one in his right. Firing at the party wall he traced a rough circle, bullets shredding the thin plaster, kicked at its centre until he broke through. He tossed his bag in to the adjoining room and clambered after it. He reloaded, grabbed a flashbang from the bag, opened the door and threw it at them. His back to the door he listened for the whump, then out, a quick glance at the team stumbling about. He evaluated the threat, decided it was minimal and ran for the stairs.

Maya sat in a holding cell gnawing her fingernails, she thought about her actions, what choice did she have? She had to betray him, they'd threatened her with thirty years in prison! Chris had killed people, he deserved to be caught. His plan to murder Marshall was pointless, he would only be replaced by another equally as ruthless, perhaps even worse.

The door opened and in came the two officers who'd arrested her. They both looked drained, the man had damp patches on his jacket and a smear of vomit on his shirt that he must have missed when cleaning up.

"Did you get him?" Maya said.

"Does it look like we got him?" Charlotte loomed over the girl, pushing her face in to Maya's, her expression angry, lips pressed together, eyes narrowed.

"I warned you that he was dangerous."

"Dangerous. I don't even know what that bloody thing was he hit us with." She still felt sick from it but at least she hadn't thrown up. Then the flashbang, blind and deaf, for what, a minute? Enough time for him to flee, no trace. She should have posted teams at the exits, but had underestimated the threat, it wouldn't look good at the review. At least there hadn't been casualties, the S.W.A.T. team's ablative vests dispersing the AP rounds causing bruises and bruised egos but no permanent damage.

Nick leant on the wall, feeling woozy, ashamed at being the only one to vomit when that thing went off. Well, it was Fuller's mess, took her down a peg or two, she wouldn't be so cocky now. The assault team commander had made it clear where the blame would be lain, about the five P's not meaning piss poor planning, his rant descending in to incoherence as the enormity of the fuck up began to sink in.

Maya shifted back on the bench, her hands clenched together.

"But I'm free to go?" She said.

"Free?" Charlotte laughed, the county was on full alert, leave cancelled and patrols increased. Her Perse mailbox full with messages from senior officers, her career in ruins unless she could resolve it quickly.

"I kept up my part, told you where he was."

"You think that's enough? You gave us nothing, not even his full name."

"I don't know it."

"Chris T. Redentor."

Maya frowned. "Then you know it, you don't need me."

"You're not going anywhere."

"You promised."

"Where's he going?"

"I don't know, he didn't tell me anything." Her voice tight and high pitched.

"I don't believe you."

"Please it's the truth." Maya looked past Charlotte at Nick, raised her hands in supplication. Embarrassed, he dropped his head.

"You're in here till we get him."

"But we had a deal."

Charlotte laughed, the sound forced and grating. Nick studied the floor wondering how he was to get the girl to Marshall. He tapped Charlotte on the shoulder.

"Can I speak to you outside?" He said.

"What?" She glanced at him, the annoyance evident on her face. She had just got started, was going to pile the pressure on the girl until she cracked.

"D.I. Fuller, can I talk to you outside?" He tapped on the

door, listened for the catch release and pushed it open. Hands on her hips, Charlotte stared at him, sighed and followed him out. She waited for him to close the cell door.

"What is it Nick?"

"This isn't going to get us anywhere."

"You've got a better suggestion?"

"We let her go."

Charlotte shook her head. "Of all the stupid..."

He held his hand up.

"Wait, let me explain."

"Go on."

"Look, it's doubtful that this Chris will contact her again."

"But possible."

"Yes, but not if she's in here."

"You suggesting we tail her?"

"Doubt we'd get the sign off for the resource, but we could put a tracker in her bag."

"She's going to lead us to him?"

"No. I don't think she'll ever see him again. But it's worth a shot, and we can always pick her back up."

"Unless she ditches the bag."

He shrugged. "There's a chance she might, I doubt it though."

"Lot of doubts."

"What's the alternative? We keep her locked up and charge her with possession?"

"And the murder of her pimp."

"We made a deal."

"You think that matters?"

"It might compromise the case, she might walk on both."

"Mights and doubts."

'More than you've got' he thought, staying silent. He watched her face, waiting for her to process the choices.

"I don't know." She said, there was something going on here, it felt wrong. She had heard rumours about Nick, comments about evidence going missing, cases falling through. But nothing concrete, nothing she could bring up before her superiors, and now she had her own shit storm to deal with, her review would be in the morning and she should be preparing her defence or at least how to pin it on someone else.

"Fine." She said, if it went wrong she'd make it known it had been Nick's plan, leave him to take the heat.

"I'll check a tracker out, stash it in her bag." He pulled out his Perse and flicked through the requisition forms, finding the relevant one he began to fill it in.

"Do that." Charlotte left him at the cell door and headed back to the office.

Nick watched her round the corner, switched his Perse to personal and typed in a message, read the reply and deleted it.

Foolish to wait for her like a love sick child, it had almost got him caught, revenge unfulfilled. Bag between his feet he sat on a bench by a fountain in the centre of a park several streets from the hotel, his head down, not engaging with the few people; dog walkers in the main, who were about at that time in the day. He checked it was clear before unlooping the machine pistol string from his neck and stuffing the guns in to the top of the bag. He rummaged through it for a beanie. Sirens echoed, disturbing the birds, drowning out the sound of the water splashing until they passed. He averted his face from a jogger and pulled the wool hat over his hair. It was obvious that Maya had betrayed him, he should have been out of the hotel the minute she had left. He lit a cigarette, leant back on the bench and closed his eyes, thinking through his next steps, weighing up the choices. They had a description now, patrols on the lookout for him, train and bus stations locked down, neighbouring counties alerted in case he tried to cross the border. What he should do is get out of the county, come back in six months if he came back at all. But that would mean Marshall got to live and he couldn't allow that. Not after all he had lost. After what it had cost him. His time was limited, he had to act, Marshall had to die, and it had to be now, do it as Cam had told him to, no fucking about.

Find him, kill him, move on.

He stood, hoisting the bag on to his shoulder, let the cigarette butt fall from his lips and ground it out with his foot. Marshall had to die, that was all that mattered now, just get it done like Cam had wanted. If he had listened to her then she would still be alive. She could have gone home instead of dying in an alley. She had come here for him, against her better judgement she had come, and he had got her killed.

He brushed at his eyes, rubbing away the tears, sniffed and spat tobacco stained phlegm on to the grass. Leaving the park he crossed the road heading further in to the town centre, stopping at a hardware shop where he bought plastic pipe, end caps, gate springs, washers and a hacksaw. Outside he went round the back of the store and, using the bins as a workbench, he sawed a length off the pipe, screwed on a cap, dropped in the washers and springs to make a suppressor. He pocketed it, reloaded the machine pistols and left the alley. On the street he checked the bus stops, looking for one that would take him to Elysium Delights.

Nick activated the tracker and opened Maya's rucksack looking for a place to hide it.

"You could split the stitching." The duty sergeant tapped her finger on a bunny ear. "Looks like it's already fraying there." She said.

"I don't want it to fall out." Nick said.

"Just push it in."

"You sound like my boyfriend."

The woman blushed and looked away. Nick smiled, teased a

thread loose with his nail opening it up and slid the tracker in to the ear. He massaged it until it was lodged at the base.

"You've done that before." The woman said.

"Little tip for you next time you're with your fella." He winked at her, laughed when her colour deepened. He put the rucksack on the counter.

"I'll be back with the girl to sign it out."

"Right." She put it in an evidence bag and dropped it in the drawer behind her.

Nick opened the cell door and motioned for Maya to come out. She stood and smoothed down the skirt, awkward with the length, its modesty hampering her motion.

"We're letting you go." He said.

"But, the other…" She let her sentence trail off.

"I spoke to her, said you weren't worth the hassle of charging." He held the door open.

"Unless you want to stay here?"

"No!" She squeezed past him and headed down the corridor, stopped when she realised she didn't know which way to go.

"Keep on." He said, catching up with her, gave her a push to get her walking again.

"I really can leave?"

"Said so didn't I?"

They approached the duty desk, Nick raised his voice.

"One to sign out Sarge."

He scrolled through his Perse bringing up the charge sheet and signed it off. He held it out to her.

"Sign."

She dragged her finger across the screen, scrawling her name. Jenkins countersigned and flicked it at the duty sergeant.

"She needs her stuff."

"OK." The woman checked through the file, confirmed it

and tapped to open the evidence drawer. She pulled out the bag and dumped it on the counter.

"Check then sign here." She said, holding out her Perse to Maya

"Of course we kept your drugs." Nick said.

She shrugged, grabbed her rucksack and signed for it without checking the contents.

"I can go?" She said.

"Yeah, off you go." He pointed to the exit.

She looked at it then back at him, not quite believing she was free, that this wasn't a trick.

"Go on." Nick gave her a push. "Get out. Don't let me see you again."

She stumbled, got her balance, turned to glare at him, resisted the temptation to tell him to fuck himself. She was free, just get out of there.

Outside she paused on the steps, rummaged in her bag for a cigarette, swore at her depleted cash, only a few low denomination notes remaining from what Chris had given her. She spat on the threshold.

"That's what got you mixed up in all this in the first place."

A man approached her, slim, wearing a suit shiny at the knees and elbows, brown hair slicked back from a hatchet face, sunglasses hiding weak eyes.

"What?" She fished out a pack, put a cigarette between her lips.

"Spitting. Dirty habit." He held up a lighter.

She bent her head accepting the flame.

"I know you?" She said.

"I don't think I've had the pleasure." He looked her up and down, traced his tongue across his lips. "Yet."

She held the disgust from her face, blew smoke. "You a cop?" She said, thinking about entrapment.

"Do I look like a cop?"

"We're in front of a cop shop and you're propositioning me."
"Propositioning? No, no. But you are coming with me."
"Why?" She backed away from him. "Who are you?"
"The names Stoker, but that's not important."
"Oh, and what is?"
"That I work for Mr Marshall, and he wants a word."

"No." She made to turn, to head back in to the police station, saw Nick standing in the entrance staring at her, held her arms out to him. Stoker grabbed her shoulder, pulled her back, jabbed his fist in to her kidney causing her to cry out in pain.

A limo pulled up at the kerb, Stoker dragged her down the steps, opened the rear door and pushed her in. She stumbled, fell face first on to the carpet, heard the door slam and tried to get to her feet, felt hands under her armpits hoisting her on to the seat.

"Mr Marshall, please." She said, realised he wasn't in the car, confused she looked round the empty interior.

"Mr Marshall?"

Stoker sat beside her, his smile a twisted leer.

"You think he'd waste his time waiting here for you?"

"Then, what?" She shuddered with fear, tried to open the door, found it locked.

"He has some questions for you."

"I'll tell him everything."

"I know you will, they always do."

She shook, she had heard about the house, the girls who went to one of his parties and didn't return. She was going to piss herself, Marshall would kill her, she should have stayed with Chris, she should have never gone with Chris, she should have taken her beating from Lennon, she shouldn't have cried out. She didn't want to die, she wanted to live, anything, she would do anything.

"Please, let me go." She held her hand out, touched his leg, rubbed her hand along it.

He smiled, moved in to her, leant to whisper in her ear.

"After, when he's done with you."

She whimpered, her hand dropping limp, he laughed moving away to tap on the smoked privacy glass that separated them from the driver.

The car moved off, she felt urine soak through her skirt and into the leather.

Minus Two

Another hotel room, indistinguishable from the many they had slept in, Cam preferring chains for their standard layout, no unpleasant surprises or even pleasant ones. John woke first and rolled over to face her. She lay on her back, mouth partially open, a light susurrating snore. He slipped from under the duvet and pulled on a thick cotton robe, belting it around his waist on the way to the bathroom. Coming back out he glanced at the bed, she had shifted on to her side, away from him, head half under the pillow. He slumped down on a chair in front of the Ent, read the time twisting above the dais and muttered instructions to bring up a room service menu.

He showered, letting the hot water pummel him, a welcome change from dips in the sea and a gravity fed rinse after with water heated by the sun. Stepping out of the stall he heard the door chime, dried off and put the robe back on.

It chimed again, making Cam groan and pull the duvet over her face, he shook his head at her, a half smile at her actions, checked the screen and opened the door. Outside a waiter stood besides a trolley.

"Room service sir."

"That's fine, I'll take it." John tapped a bank card on the pad and pulled the trolley in to the room.

He poured out two cups of coffee, adding milk and sugar to his and carried them over to the bed.

"Cam?"

"Where's my fucking coffee?"

"Always the same greeting."

She smiled, pushed up to lean back against the headboard, ran fingers through her hair sweeping it back from her face.

"Not much longer."

John handed her a cup, his expression hard to read. He stared at her for a moment, nodded and said.

"So that's it then? When you're done, we're done too?"

"You're too young to retire John, you've got the world to experience."

He sipped his drink, put it down on the bedside table, picked up the pack of cigarettes and took out two. He lit them both and put one between her lips. She grunted and inhaled, the tip glowing bright, a plume of smoke from her nose.

"You can come and visit." She said around it.

"Visit? What for a fuck holiday?"

She sucked her teeth, tapped ash into the ashtray. "I'm sure there'll be some fucking."

He said nothing, took a long pull on his cigarette and ground it out. His face fierce, anger causing him to clamp his jaw shut, fear holding back the words he wanted to say.

She smiled, focused on the end of her cigarette, the bright glow turning to ash, sucked it back to life, drank from her cup and put it down besides his.

"You're quiet." She said, thinking of the boy she had watched become a man, that she had made into a thief and killer, taken his life and made it into hers.

"I sometimes wonder what's the point of it all."

She tsked. "I've told you, there isn't any."

He shook his head, unwilling to accept her outlook, there must be a reason, they weren't just filling time till they died.

"Live in the moment John, embrace beauty when you see it, realise that nothing lasts."

"Embrace beauty?" He took her cigarette and added it to the

ashtray, leant in to kiss her.

She laughed and pulled him onto the bed.

Munching a piece of toast, Detective Sergeant Nick Jenkins sat at his breakfast bar and contemplated the outcome of the latest bet he had placed, this time on a horse race in Japan. The resultant debt glowed an angry red on his Perse's screen, the amount enough to make him feel sick, thoughts of the consequences of not paying it, the price asked of him instead. He dropped the toast on to a plate and slid off the elevated stool, padded across the carpeted area of his dining kitchen and pushed his feet in to brown laced brogues. A quick check in the mirror showed a man in his early thirties, black hair tousled in a cut better suited to someone ten years younger, brown eyes in a clean shaven face, nose a straight line down the middle highlighting the asymmetry. He unhooked his car keys from the pegs by the door. His Perse vibrated, the strident beat of Chanks's latest starting to build, he glanced at the display, frowned and answered it.

"Jenkins."

"This is Marshall."

"Mr Marshall, how are you?"

"Cut the shit, you got my money?"

"I can get it Mr Marshall, I just need some time."

"Heard that before."

"Mr Marshall."

"Got a way for you to dent a corner on it."

Nick twisted the keyfob in his hand, waited for the man to continue.

"Well?"

"If I can Mr Marshall, I mean if it's something I can do."

"I've got business on Saint Verity this morning around eleven, keep your lot away."

"Away?"

"Yeah, away, in case it gets noisy."

"How noisy?"

"As noisy as it gets." The man disconnected.

Jenkins sighed and dropped the phone back in to his pocket. Noisy? What did that even mean? Verity wasn't the busiest part of town but there would still be people around at that time of day, how was he expected to stop them calling the police if something kicked off?

His Perse vibrated. He checked the screen, a hot tip on the dogs, he tapped putting five hundred on, cursed at the time and left his flat making sure the door locked behind him.

On the drive to Sharpe's Gun Emporium Cam mulled over John's plan or rather lack of one. Car bomb, what was he thinking? The Sons had left their mark on him, given him a predilection for the extreme. But then it would achieve its aim and she had done far worst in the past for the sake of expedience. It was his call, her job in this was backup, muscle, follow his play and try to get them out alive at the end of it.

They turned on to Verity and passed the shop without slowing.

"You've missed it." John said.

"Yes." She took the second left and stopped the car.

John scowled. "Why here? We could have parked outside the shop."

"I'm getting a vibe."

"A vibe? I thought you didn't believe in all that."

"I don't, but sometimes it's best to heed it."

John sighed, they had been together for eight years and still she came out with this nonsense.

"So we have to carry the stuff back here?"

"I am sure he will put them in a bag." She said, getting out the car. She waited for him to exit and blipped it locked.

"Which I will be carrying."

"Do you good, you're getting chubby." She winked as she said it taking some of the sting out. He sighed again, followed her along the road back to the shop.

"What's your vibe telling you?" He said.

"This all feels..." She stopped, looked up and down the street. "Wrong."

"Wrong?"

"I don't like it, the street's too quiet."

"It's ten am. Everyone's at work."

"Maybe." She continued walking. "I didn't care for that man, Sharpe."

John laughed. "Because he called you madam?"

She glowered and flicked her cigarette at him, he battered it away.

"Watch it." He said.

"I was thinking the same."

She opened the door of the gun shop and held it for him.

"Thanks." He muttered. Knowing she was sending him in as bait, he zipped up his jacket hoping its bullet resistant claims weren't marketing hyperbole. He checked the interior, a visual sweep of corners and ambush points. Satisfied he held two fingers up behind his back, dropped them. She followed him in and let the door swing shut.

Sharpe was sitting behind the counter, he stood and placed his hands on the top. An attempt at a smile failing, the man looked nervous, worried.

"Ah, Ms. Malone, and uh, associate, you're early."

"Early birds to catch Mr Sharpe."

"Right." Processing her reply he looked puzzled, let it slide and gestured at a stack of boxes on the counter.

"Everything you requested." He held out his Perse to her, the thumb scanner pulsing in anticipation.

"If you would like to settle your bill?" He said.

Cam rested her hand on top of the packages.

"I'd like to check them first."

Sharpe stuttered. "Of course, of course." He had hoped she would pay for them before Marshall's men picked her up, enabling him to keep the weapons and her money.

Cam opened the first, taking out the vests. Noting the kitemark she said. "British?"

"Of course."

She nodded. "They will have to do."

Returning them to their box she checked through the rest of the items.

"These magazines are empty."

"We are not allowed to sell them any other way. As you can see I have put in cartons of the requested ammunition."

"I want them loading."

"It's the law, there is nothing I can do about it."

"Then I won't be buying them."

"I put myself at quite a disadvantage if I give you loaded guns."

"You're at a big fucking disadvantage as it is, I don't need a gun to fuck you over, you want your money you load them."

Sharpe shrank back from her, glanced at the time on his Perse and made a decision.

"Well if you're going to take them now then I could load them."

"Good."

He took the magazines back and slid them into the autoloader, emptied one of the cartons into the hopper on top. Fascinated John watched him start it running, cartridges were spun to orient them, lined up and and pushed in to a clip, the filled ones ejecting from the bottom. Something he could have done with in the camp, instead of the long, boring hours of loading them by hand. Cam took the first one and slid it into a pistol, chambered a round and thumbed off the safety. She pointed it at the shopkeeper.

"Ms. Malone?" Sharpe shrank away from her, his hands held palms out, his face turned away.

She smiled and placed it on the counter.

"I want the automatics loading too."

"Of course." He wiped his forehead with the back of his hand, forced a smile. He offered his Perse to her again.

"If you would like to pay?"

Cam ignored the reader, offering him a bank card instead.

"Take it from that."

"Thank you ma-Ms. Malone."

He processed the payment, waiting for the confirmation he tapped his fingers on the counter until a raised eyebrow from Cam made him stop.

"Sorry." He offered an apology. "Won't be long now."

She lit a cigarette, Sharpe glanced at the no smoking sign and back at her. She narrowed her eyes and blew smoke in to his face. He stepped back coughing, heard a confirmation ping on his Perse and handed back her card.

"All in order." His smile genuine now.

John considered the pile of weapons, he picked up a bag from a rack and started to put them in it.

"That is £14.58." Sharpe said.

Cam sucked her teeth and threw the card on to the counter. "Add it on then."

"For Christ's sake!"

Callan banged the steering wheel in frustration. He had got to the gun shop half an hour before Marshall said the couple were due and it looked like they were already leaving. He watched them pass and walk down the street.

"That them?" Benks said, sat besides him, a shotgun laid across his lap.

"I reckon, you ready?"

Benks chambered a beanbag round in response. "Ready like

Ruby."

Callan flashed the van parked in front of their car, Stoker stuck his head out of the driver's window and looked back at them. Callan pointed at the couple, made a grabbing motion, Stoker nodded and pulled away from the kerb, speeding up to overtake them. Callan started the car and drove up behind.

"What was all that about?" John said.

"Something didn't feel right, I didn't trust him."

"He seemed a bit jumpy. But you'd made him load the magazines, break the law."

"Break the law, as if anyone gives a fuck? No, I just got a vibe."

"Vibe."

John hefted the bag onto his shoulder, muttering about the weight. Cam ignored him, checking the street she lit a cigarette, a van passed and then slowed, bounced up on to the pavement.

She pulled her pistol out and spun round looking for the backup vehicle, fired into the windscreen as John emptied his magazine into the van. Callan swore and swerved, smashed into a parked car and kicked his door open rolling out onto the ground. He looked back at Benks slumped in the passenger seat, his face a bloody mess. He could see Henley and Stoker returning fire, pushing the couple back into an alley where they crouched down behind a dumpster.

"Fuck John, it's a dead end." Cam said.

Reloading he glanced over his shoulder, they were in a service alley, access doors secured with steel grilles, no windows below the first floor, with a two metre high wall at the end.

"It's climbable."

"If you're not being shot at."

She pulled a vest from the bag, handed it to John, took out

the other and put it on.

He zipped his on over his jacket and said. "We have a plan?"

She ignored him concentrating instead on loading a machine pistol.

"Cam?"

"Shush, I'm thinking." She rose in a fluid movement and sprayed a clip at their attackers, dropping back down to reload.

"I counted three, two behind the van, another on the right hand side, probably from the car, must have killed the driver."

"Three of them then, with machine guns."

The bin shuddered and bucked, absorbing the rounds, stench of garbage filling the air. John stood and returned fire emptying the pistol, he crouched, letting the magazine drop free.

"We could drag the dumpster down the alley then use it to get over the wall." He said.

She passed him a magazine. "That's your plan?"

"You have a better one?"

"No."

She rocked the slide back, stood, pistol coming up, shuddered and spun, collapsed to the ground.

"Cam!" John screamed, he grabbed her shoulders dragging her behind the bin, his arms around her, he held her up, her head resting on his chest.

"The cunt, what the fuck?" She poked at the holes in her vest, stared at the blood on her fingers.

"I think, shit, I think. We keep the receipt?"

She laughed, dropped back against him.

"Cam?"

"Fuck." More a mutter, she tried to move, her legs numb, a black veil creeping over her vision.

"Fuck."

"Cam?" He squeezed her to him, his voice a whisper in her ear. She felt cold, the lack of pain a worry, meant it was serious, she wouldn't be walking away from this. Her stump itched, scolding her for being an idiot. She had known it was a fool's mission, they should have left it, never come back to this place, stayed on Koh Tansey. Hot coffee in the mornings, sex and cigarettes, the sound of waves soothing you to sleep. Not here, bleeding to death in an alley.

They should have left it, this country had been nothing but a curse to her.

And now John, he had to leave her, he was dead if he didn't.

"John, this is it, give me the pistols, I'll provide cover."

"What?" He gripped her harder, his face wet with tears, she raised her hand, let it fall before she touched him.

"John, you have to leave me, run."

"Cam, no, no. You'll be OK, just hold on, we'll get out of this, please Cam."

"John, there's too much damage, I can't feel my legs, this is it. You have to run, leave me."

"Cam, no, I can't leave you."

"Then we're both dead, and for nothing!"

"Cam, I can't."

He kissed her, the taste of her blood on his lips.

"I'll hold them off, provide cover, you have to go John." She fumbled at her throat undid the charm necklace and pushed it into his hands.

"Cam."

"Don't Cam me, don't beg or whine, now give me the guns and run."

Ten

"You know that place on Ethel?"

"No, I don't think so." Stew shuffled his feet, stared down at them. Tyler smiled, brushed a loose strand of hair behind an ear.

"Yeah it's a..." Her voice trailed off, attention shifting to the man walking up the road towards the guardhouse. He stopped in front of them and dropped a bag, his right arm coming up.

"Shit!" Tyler said going for her gun.

He shot her in the face, the dull phutt confusing Stew, he was a big man, but his experience of violence was limited to fists and baseball bats. When Mr Marshall had given him a pistol he had needed Tyler's help to take the safety off. She'd teased him for that, asked him about a few other things, his shoe size being of particular interest to her. They'd been getting on and he'd been mustering up the courage to ask her about getting a drink after the shift ended. He looked at her body slumped on the ground, then at her assailant, a cocky young prick, holdall by his feet, gun pointing at Stew, something plastic stuck on the end, smoke drifting from a jagged hole.

"You killed her." Stew said, raising his arms up.

"Get in the hut."

"You killed her."

"Are you fucking simple mate? Get in the hut."

"You killed her!" He roared the last, jumping towards the

man, the first round striking his chest, three more punching him back, his foot catching on Tyler's body he collapsed on top of her.

"Tyler." He touched her hair and closed his eyes.

"Fuck." Standing over him the man said. "You're going to be a cunt to move."

Followed by Stoker, Marshall walked in to the room where they had shackled her naked to a chair. He ripped the hood from her head and said.

"Maya is it?"

Her face twisted with fear, she tried to shrink back from him. "Please Mr Marshall, I don't know anything."

"You killed Lennon."

"No, that was him, Chris, he did it."

She shook, head down, focussing on the floor, her trembling making the chains round her ankles rattle, leather bands holding her arms behind her back. He gripped her chin forcing her to look up at him.

"You asked him?"

"No, I, I didn't, well I shouted but I didn't think he would, I didn't think he would do that, kill Lennon I mean."

"Shush." He ran a finger down her cheek.

"If you tell me the truth then you will be OK, are you going to tell me the truth?"

He would give her to the men and then the pigs after.

"Please Mr Marshall, I'll tell you everything, please don't hurt me."

"Who is this man?"

"He said his name was Chris, the cops, they said it was Chris Redentor, Chris T."

"Chris T Redentor?"

"That's what they said, Chris T Redentor."

"And this was the man who did over my bookies?"

"Yes, and..." She bit her lip, tried to look away. He pressed his fingers into her flesh, manicured nails cutting half moon indentations.

"And what?"

"The money place, where the pimps take their money."

He squeezed harder, leant down to hold his face close to hers.

"And how did he find that?" His voice low, the words filled with menace.

She squirmed, tried to break his grip, failed and stuttered her reply.

"I don't know Mr Marshall, I don't know."

"We'll see." He twisted her head towards the cabinets on the wall, instruments visible behind the glass fronts. He let go of her and straightened up, turned to Stoker standing by the door.

"Fasten her hand."

Stoker grinned, his walk over to Maya a cocky swagger, imagining what was about to happen his smile became a leer. He bent to unbound her left arm, twisting it round, her struggles futile, unable to prevent him jamming her fingers in to the rings welded to the table.

Marshall held a pair of bolt cutters in front of her face.

"How many fingers till I get the truth?"

"Mr Marshall, please no, I'll tell you anything, please."

"Did he mention Cam?"

"Cam Mr Marshall?"

"Yes, did he mention her?"

"No, I don't know who that is."

Marshall ran the cutters down her arm tracing a wavy line, at her hand he opened them and set the jaws round her little finger.

"Did he mention Cam?"

"Please Mr Marshall." She began to cry, gasping for breath, fear overwhelming her, panicking at the sight of the bolt cutters, trying to pull her hand free. Stoker grinned and held it down, stared into her eyes wanting to see the pain there.

"What did he say about Cam."

He tightened his grip cutting the skin.

She yelped. "Please Mr Marshall, don't hurt me, please, I will tell you anything you want, please, don't, please."

"What did he say about Cam?"

"Cam, Mr Marshall, Cam, he didn't mention a Cam. Who is Cam?"

He squeezed the bolt cutters shut snipping the finger off. Maya screamed in pain, Stoker laughed and punched her in the jaw. Stunned her head lolled forward, she mumbled, her words unintelligible, her eyes unfocused. She pulled her hand free, touched her face catching the stump on her chin. She screamed again.

Marshall picked up the amputated finger and tossed it in to a steel waste-basket.

"Back on the table." He said.

"No, please no."

She pushed at Stoker trying to break his grip. "Please Mr Marshall."

"If you want to keep at least a couple of fingers then you will tell me what I want to know."

"That's all I know, he didn't talk much, he didn't tell me anything."

Her piss dripped from the slatted chair, the gutter beneath channelling it to the sluice in the corner.

"That's a pity for you then, fasten her hand."

He bypassed the main gate and scaled the wall, dropping into the grounds. He opened his bag and took out the machine pistols, hanging them back around his neck, stuffed the remaining magazines into his pockets. He left the bag and crouch walked to the house, avoiding the front entrance and looking for another way in. His feet clanged on something, he looked down at a manhole cover, no, a coal chute, access into the cellar. He checked it, smiling at the memory, almost relieved to discover it was now welded shut, and moved on to the window. He smashed the glass with the butt of his gun, running it round the edge to remove any shards and stepped inside. An alarm wailed heralding his arrival, he checked the room, an expensive Ent with chairs around it. A bookcase against one wall, a large fireplace, rugs on a polished wood floor, a single door that took him out in to the hall. The next room had a bed in the centre surrounded by screens and medical equipment. Was Marshall injured, perhaps even dying? He raised a pistol and approached it, placed his hand on a screen and was about to pull it aside when he heard movement behind him. He spun, fired a burst, dropped and rolled coming up on his knees and emptied the rest of the clip in to Henley, who fell backwards, shotgun skittering on the floor. He raised his left pistol, thumb on the right releasing the clip, dropping it free. Letting it hang on the string he pulled a magazine out and slotted it home.

"And you would be Chris?" A voice called out to him, even after eight years he recognised the sardonic tone, the lazy drawl.

"Marshall." He shuffled over to the wall by the door, glanced through the opening.

"You come for your whore?"

"I've come for you." He zipped up his jacket and tucked the automatic in to the small of his back.

"Over what? A woman? Let's sit down and work something out."

"I have nothing to say to you, I'm going to kill you."

"Chris, don't be foolish. You're trapped." Hearing the alarm Marshall had left Maya chained to the chair, entering the hall in time to see Henley gunned down. He was now pressed against the cellar doorway, a pistol in his hand. Behind him Stoker stood similarly armed. Holding a SMG, Callan crouched by the main door, using an elephant foot umbrella stand for cover.

"Go back down." Marshall whispered to Stoker. "Come round the other side and we'll box him in."

Stoker nodded and disappeared down the stairs.

"Chris, we can work this out. Nothing done that can't be fixed."

"Fixed?"

"Yes, you didn't know who you were dealing with, you made a mistake. Make amends and you can walk away."

"A mistake?"

"Yes, and I must say you've impressed me, I'd be willing to give you a job, let you work it off."

"Work it off?"

"That's right."

"Why would I work for a cunt like you?"

"Now Chris, there's no need for that."

"You killed my parents you fucker."

"I don't..."

"You killed my parents!" He shouted, firing both machine pistols he ran in to the hall. Shells clattered on the parquet flooring, pistol slides locking open he let go of them, pulled out his automatic. Two shots dropping Callan. Marshall fired at him, a round striking his shoulder, his gun falling from numbed fingers.

"You'll have to do better than that." He shouted, drawing his knife and slashing forwards, cutting Marshall's wrist, causing him to drop his weapon, following through the move to come up behind, a choke hold, weak but effective, the tanto's tip resting under Marshall's eye.

"You killed my parents." His voice breaking on the last word.

"We can sort this out." Marshall clasped his left hand over the wound.

"Going to bring them back are you?"

"I didn't kill your parents."

"Don't lie to me." He sliced a line across Marshall's cheek.

"Name like Redentor would have stuck in my mind."

"Try McPhereson."

"What?"

"My name is John McPhereson."

"And I killed your parents?"

"Eight years ago."

The blade cut deeper, Marshall tried to tilt his head back from the point.

"Eight years, you expect me to remember?"

"I remember."

"We can work something out, I have money."

John raised his left arm, rattled the charms in Marshall's face.

"I have your money, I have all the fucking money I need."

"Cam, then, I have…"

Her name brought it all back, the past eight years, the killing and stealing building towards this, his revenge for his parents. To this moment, this was it and it felt like ashes in his mouth.

He laughed.

"Something funny John?"

"I thought I would feel something, more than this anyway."

He sliced through Marshall's throat and let the body fall.

Minus One

Nick pulled up at the end of the street killing the siren but leaving the lights flashing. He cancelled the rest of the response, ticking the raised in error box and adding a comment about hoax call before submitting it. He could see Callan pressed to the wall by the entrance to an alley, a van up on the pavement, two men crouched behind it and another car blocking the road, the windscreen smashed.

"What the fuck are you doing?" He got out of his car and walked over to Callan.

The man jolted in surprise, recognised the DS and lowered his SMG. He gestured at the alleyway.

"We got them trapped down there."

"This isn't Oxford, you can't have a gun fight in the middle of the day and it not be reported!"

"Marshall said get them, no matter what."

Nick checked his Perse, relieved there were no new incidents raised he dropped it back in his pocket.

"Look's like you got away with it." He glanced at the car. "You need to move that, traffic's light but people will want to get past."

"We need to get them first."

"Go get them then."

"They've got guns."

"I can't hear any shooting."

Callan shrugged. "They could be playing dead, waiting for

us."

"Don't you think you should check?"

"Why don't you?"

Callan's Perse chirped, he glanced at it and cursed.

"Marshall is coming, he's five minutes away."

"Better check then hadn't you?"

"Be my guest."

"I don't work for you."

He stared at Callan. Belligerent, the man returned it.

"Who you think he'll blame?" Nick said.

"Shit." Callan looked away, waved over at the men to get their attention. He pointed at the alleyway.

"Henley, go and see."

"Why the fuck should I?"

"Marshall will be here in five minutes."

"Fuck."

Henley checked his gun then ran hunched over to the alley entrance. He stuck his arm round and fired a shot, pulled it back in and waited.

"Mike." Callan said.

"Oh fuck." He clenched the weapon to his chest, his back pressed against the wall.

"I won't tell you again."

"Fuck."

Henley raised his gun and stepped in to the alleyway, he fired a burst, bullets ricocheting off the walls.

"Keep it down you idiot." Nick pulled out his Perse ready to cancel fresh alerts.

Henley reloaded, dashed up to the dumpster and crouched behind it. He waited, getting his nerve up.

"Marshall will be here soon Mike."

"Fuck." Crab walking he edged round the side of the bin, gun up, ready to shoot, almost firing when he spotted Cam lying slumped against the wall, head down, eyes closed, a machine pistol on the ground next to her.

"Hey Callan?"

"Yes?"

"The woman's here, lot of blood."

"The other one?"

"No sign."

"She dead?"

"Not sure, she's not moving."

"Find out, Marshall's car just pulled up."

"Fuck."

Henley kicked the gun out of reach. He prodded her with his foot eliciting a groan. "She's alive. Shall I off her?"

"Wait."

Callan ran to the limo and opened the rear door, standing back as Marshall got out.

"You got her?" The man said.

"Yes, Mr Marshall, she's just down there."

"Why are you all here then?"

"Just checking she's not a danger."

"Danger?"

"She was armed, Henley's checking it out now."

"I said I wanted her alive."

"They started shooting first."

Marshall grabbed Callan by the lapel and pulled him close.

"She's no good to me dead."

"She's not, she's alive." Callan tried to back away, panicked he looked over his shoulder to shout to Henley.

"Mike, she still alive?"

"Yeah? Shall I off her?"

Marshall pushed Callan out of his way and approached the alley.

"She dies and I won't be happy, you understand?"

"Crystal Mr Marshall." Henley called back, looked at the woman and swore under his breath, wondered if he should do something to stop the bleeding.

"You done your job?" Marshall said to Nick.

"Yes, we won't be bothered."

"Good."

Marshall walked down the alley. Taking care to avoid the pooling blood he hitched his trousers up and squatted beside Cam, reached out and slapped her cheek.

"It's Marshall, do you remember me Cam?"

"John?" She moved her head, tried to raise a hand.

"John, who's that? Your fuck buddy?"

"John, I told you to run."

"He won't get far." He ran his fingers over her face, gripped her chin and twisted her head towards him.

"John, I, John."

"Where's my money Cam?"

"John, my name is Maelea."

"I don't give a fuck what your name is, where is my money?"

"Get away John, you need to run."

Marshall stood up and motioned to one of his men.

"She's not making any sense, take her back to my house, don't let her die till she tells me where my money is."

Pistol clenched in his hand, John dropped from the wall and ran out of the alley in to the road. He increased his pace, desperate to be away from where she lay dying, the shame of abandoning her driving him on. Catching a toe on raised paving, he stumbled and went sprawling, turned it in to a forward roll and regained his feet.

Chest heaving from the exertion he slowed his pace, fighting the urge to run, common sense knowing that he should walk, be inconspicuous, just someone out shopping.

Normal, nothing out of the ordinary, just slip away unnoticed.

Conscious of the automatic, he unzipped the ablative vest to get to the shoulder holster.

Useless fucking thing!

He shrugged it off and threw it in to the street, zipped his jacket up. He tried to think, but it was all mixed up in his head. He had left her there to die, she had told him to run, she was dying, but still.

He had left her.

Marshall had taken everything from him, first his parents and now Cam. She had warned him not to come here, he hadn't listened and she had paid the price. This was all his fault, it was all Marshall's fault, he would make him pay.

But how?

He lit a Puretone, blew out smoke, looked for a street sign, some indication of where he was in the town. He had little cash and a gun, he needed to get back to the car but not yet, give it time to settle down. Wait till the police had been and cleared up the scene, wait till they had removed...

Wait till they had removed the body.

His legs buckled and he leant against a wall.

"Get a grip." He muttered. "Come on John, get a grip."

The words making him think of her, bringing comfort and pain combined.

"OK." He rubbed his eyes, pushing the tears away, for now. "OK."

Marshall's brazen assault in the day gave credence to his claim that he owned the cops, he would have to find some way to divert them. There was still the option of killing the Mayor but the set up would take too long, he needed to finish this, Marshall had to die, not just for his parents but for Cam as well. She had warned him, told him to leave it. He had thought she didn't care for him, all she wanted was to sit by the sea, be done with it all. He hadn't understood, he had pushed her, made her come back here. She would rub her stump whenever he mentioned it, tell him to leave revenge for the fools. But in the end she had come with him, and at what cost? Now he was alone, Marshall had won and he didn't even know it. Eight years of killing and stealing, eight wasted years when he could have had a life, a real life, family, someone who loved him as much as he loved her. She had though, never said it but shown him in the end, come here for him, died in an alley for him.

He lit a cigarette from the stub of the last, returning the packet to his pocket his hand brushed the necklace. He pulled it free, oblivious to the tears streaming down his face he touched the charms that hung from it. This was no good, blubbing in the street, he needed to focus, she would have laughed in his face, told him to suck it up, channel the pain, make it someone else's.

Marshall had to pay, he owed it to Cam to finish the job, make her death have not been for nothing. He wrapped the chain twice around his left wrist and fastened it, flicked his cigarette into the gutter. He made up his mind, he would rob a bank, make it bloody, give the cops something to chase, leave Marshall vulnerable, weak. Bring his world down around him, take everything from him.

Then he would kill him.

Acknowledgements

I'd like to thank Adam Preston for his diligent spotting of wonts, which while infuriating to him was a boon to me (and all the other typos he picked up on, much appreciated A.P.E.). Also Catherine Williams for her keen eye and excellent feedback, Monty for getting over the perceived slight in not letting him read it first, and Adam Tweddle for some insightful comments I chose to ignore. ☺

Printed in Great Britain
by Amazon